Eglantine

a ghost story

W9-BLD-230

CATHERINE JINKS was born in Brisbane in 1963 and grew up in Sydney and Papua New Guinea. She studied medieval history at university, and her love of reading led her to become a writer. She lives in the Blue Mountains in New South Wales with her Canadian husband and her daughter, Hannah.

Catherine Jinks is the author of over twenty books for children and adults, including the award-winning Pagan series.

120050602909

Eglantine

a ghost story

Catherine Jinks

ALLEN&UNWIN

LORETO NORMANHURST
LEARNING RESOURCE CENTRE

To Ursula Dubosarsky, who planted the seed

With special thanks to Janine Bellamy and
PRISM International

First published in 2002

Copyright © Text, Catherine Jinks 2002
Copyright © Illustrations, Steven Hunt 2002

All rights reserved. No part of this book may be reproduced or transmitted
in any form or by any means, electronic or mechanical, including
photocopying, recording or by any information storage and retrieval
system, without prior permission in writing from the publisher.
The *Australian Copyright Act 1968* (the Act) allows a maximum of one chapter or
ten per cent of this book, whichever is the greater, to be photocopied by any
educational institution for its educational purposes provided that the
educational institution (or body that administers it) has given a
remuneration notice to Copyright Agency Limited (CAL) under the Act.

Allen & Unwin
83 Alexander St
Crows Nest NSW 2065
Australia
Phone: (61 2) 8425 0100
Fax: (61 2) 9906 2218
Email: info@allenandunwin.com
Web: www.allenandunwin.com

National Library of Australia
Cataloguing-in-Publication entry:
Jinks, Catherine, 1963– .
Eglantine: a ghost story
For children.

ISBN 1 86508 844 7.

1. Ghost stories. I. Title.

A823.3

Cover and text design by Jo Hunt
Cover image by Steve Hunt, Pigs Might Fly Productions
Set in 13 on 15.5pt Weiss by Midland Typesetters
Printed in Australia by McPherson's Printing Group

2 4 6 8 10 9 7 5 3 1

Chapter One

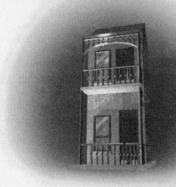

It happened after we bought this house.

I couldn't believe that Mum was serious, at first. She'd been going on and on about how wonderful it was, how it had been built in 1886, how it still had its slate roof and two original marble fire-places . . . that kind of thing. But then, when we got out of the car, we came face to face with this dump. (Half of its windows were boarded up!) It was a terrace house, squashed between two other terrace houses, with a tiny patch of front garden and a sign out the front that said 'For Sale'. Only it wasn't for sale any more.

Mum and Ray had bought it.

'Needs a bit of work,' said Mum as she opened

the front door. 'Look, kids! Look at the lovely patterns on the ceiling! I'm going to have all that linoleum taken up, and the floorboards polished. And everything will be painted, of course.'

Bethan sniffed. 'It stinks,' he offered.

'Well, that's because there were squatters living here for a while. But the smell will go.' Mum turned to Ray. 'I've aligned the *bagua*,' she said, 'and the Gate of Chi is in six, so that's okay. In fact the whole alignment's pretty good.'

Ray nodded. I should explain that while Mum may work in a bank part time, she's also an artist's model, and does some tarot reading on the side. What I mean is, she's a bit of a hippy. And she believes in all that Feng Shui stuff, where your house has to be arranged properly, for good luck.

I'm not sure if I believe in it or not.

'The kitchen's a disaster,' she said, leading us down the hall. 'We can live with the bathroom, but not the kitchen. I think I'll have the whole lot ripped out and replaced.' She said that the stove would have to be moved, because it was right next to the refrigerator – a placement that would cause 'danger and conflict'. Unless, perhaps, she put a plant between the fridge and the stove, to allow a smoother flow of energy from water to wood to fire? But that still wouldn't cure the bad placement, because the stove was sitting under the window.

'No,' she said. 'I think we'd better start from scratch. After all, a kitchen is the symbolic source of wealth and wellbeing in any house. We can't afford to get it wrong.'

No comment from me. Bethan remarked that the kitchen smelled like the old man at the railway station, and wondered aloud if *he* could have been living here. Ray wanted to know where his studio would be.

Ray is an artist, so he needs space to paint in. Mum met him when she was modelling for a life-drawing class, about five years ago. She likes his work because it's not just a bunch of squiggles and splodges and abstract shapes. She says that abstract shapes create an environment in which people find it hard to finish things. Ray paints people and houses and fruit and chairs, but not trees. He spends forty hours a week drawing trees for the Department of Forestry, so he won't paint them in his spare time.

Before Ray there was Simon, and before Simon there was my dad. But Dad lives in Thailand, now. He phones us about once a month.

'Are the bedrooms upstairs?' I asked, because the bedrooms were what really interested me. The main reason we'd decided to move in the first place was so that Bethan and I could have our own rooms. No eleven-year-old girl should be forced to

3

share a bedroom with her eight-year-old brother.

'Yes, the bedrooms are upstairs,' Mum replied. 'Yours is the one at the back, and Bethan's is the little one next to the bathroom. You go up, if you like – I'll just show Ray his studio.'

Ray's studio was a kind of shed in the back yard; Mum said that it had 'a lot of potential'. Upstairs, there were three bedrooms and a bathroom, all sitting one behind the other. The big front bedroom was for Mum and Ray, because it was the nicest, with glass doors opening onto a balcony. The bedroom at the back wasn't as nice, or as big, but it had a view of some trees out the window.

I was standing there, wondering who had painted the whole room red (yuk!) and who had left a suspicious-looking pile of rags in one corner, when Bethan called out.

'Allie! Come and look at this!'

I'd better admit, right here and now, that Allie is short for Alethea. Alethea Gebhardt – that's my name. Alethea means 'truth' in Greek, and Bethan means 'life' in Welsh.

Like I said, Mum's a bit of a hippy.

'Wow,' I said, when I reached Bethan's room. It was little and dingy, and it was covered with writing. There was writing scrawled all over the walls, the ceiling and the windowsills; only the dirty, shaggy old carpet had been spared. It wasn't the usual sort

4

of graffiti you see around the place, either. It looked as if it had been written with a pen – not spray-painted – and it was neat and small and dense.

So dense was it, in fact, that you couldn't read most of it. Lines had been scribbled over other lines, layer upon layer of script. You could only vaguely tell that it was writing at all.

From a distance, the walls appeared almost black.

'Gee,' I said.

'Is yours like this?' Bethan inquired.

'Nope. Mine's red.'

'Red writing?'

'Red paint.'

'Why do I have to get the weird one?' Bethan complained.

'It's no big deal, Bethan. We'll just paint over the writing.'

'I still don't think it's fair.'

When Mum saw the room, she said that the squatters who had lived in it must have been on drugs. Then she told Bethan not to worry, because the next time he walked into his room its walls would be white, its floor would be polished, and its energy would be very positive. Give her a month, she said, and we wouldn't know the place.

Well, she was wrong. Six weeks passed, and she

was still fighting with tradesmen and poring over laminex catalogues. She was always going off to visit the new house, and bringing back things she found there. Once she brought back scraps of ancient newspaper from under the old linoleum. Once she brought back a dirty blue bottle. (She said it was an antique.) The best thing she brought back was a book, which had been shoved under one of the stair-treads for extra support. (The stairs also needed repairing.) It was a copy of *Idylls of the King* by Alfred, Lord Tennyson – a book of poetry – and it was mouldy and speckled and eaten up by rats (or perhaps cockroaches). But you could still read bits of it, including the inscription on the fly-leaf. Someone had written, *Eglantine Higgins, 1906,* and underneath had scrawled, *A good book is the precious life-blood of a master spirit, embalmed and treasured up on purpose to a life beyond life. – Milton.*

We kept it for a while, that book, but we don't have it any more. We got rid of it because . . . Well, you'll see why. You'll see why when I tell you what happened after we finally moved in.

Our possessions were transferred on a Tuesday. When Mum picked us up from school and brought us to the new house, all our furniture was neatly arranged, although most of the boxes still had to be unpacked. The walls downstairs were white and yellow; upstairs, they were all white. The floors gleamed. There was glass in every window. The kitchen looked great, with polished wooden cupboards and clay-coloured tiles on the floor. Mum had made new curtains and hung them in the bedrooms. Even our cat, Salema, seemed happy with the change.

I went straight to my own room and lay for a while, glorying in the privacy. It was *my* room. Mine. No longer would I have to put up with Bethan's speedway set and football posters. No longer would I have to protect my Derwent pencils and animal skulls from Bethan's prying friends.

Then I heard him complaining, and went to see what was wrong.

'Look,' he said.

His room had been transformed. It was all white, and seemed much bigger, despite the cardboard boxes piled everywhere. Of course, Bethan had already begun to strew his Lego and dinosaurs about. Soon the floor would be impassable.

He's always been a messy boy.

'Look,' he said again, and pointed.

Down near the foot of his bed, along the top of the skirting board, I could see a line of script. *Once there lived in a bleak clime a white-bearded king*, it said. You could hardly make it out, but Bethan was most offended.

'The painters missed a bit,' I remarked patiently.

'What's the problem?'

'The problem is that I don't want it there!'

'So tell Mum. She'll paint over it. She's got left-over paint, remember?'

He stumped off to summon help, and Ray came up and dabbed a bit of white paint over the troublesome graffiti. We all thought that the problem had been solved. But the next morning, Bethan came down to breakfast grumbling about another missed bit, near the ceiling, above the window. He was quite worked up about it. When I stuck my head into his bedroom, however, I could barely see the writing from the door; it was the faintest grey smudge, impossible to read. I asked him why it bothered him so much.

'Because it does,' he said.

'You can't even read it.'

'I still don't want it there.'

'Why not?'

'Because this is *my bedroom*.'

My brother is very stubborn. He has red hair and freckles, like my mum, but he's stubborn like my grandmother. When he decides that he doesn't like something, there's no way you'll change his mind – not ever. So there's no use trying to convince him that books can be more fun than football magazines, or that a little bit of writing won't spoil a whole bedroom.

He'd decided that he didn't want the ravings of some loony squatter soiling his beautiful white walls. (And you can understand his point of view, I suppose.) So poor old Ray had to climb up a ladder, that evening, and paint over the words *His realm was wide enough, indeed.* Bethan went to bed much happier, as a result.

But the next morning he discovered, not one, but two more missed spots. *Many rugged mountains crossed the kingdom* had been written under the windowsill. *A barren soil and chilly sky made it seem poor* was tucked behind the wardrobe. With a sigh, Ray had to haul out the white paint again.

It was Thursday before Mum finally began to get suspicious.

'Wait a minute,' she said, peering at the line that was written directly over Bethan's bed. (*Among these were great mines of salt and iron ore.*) 'Wait just a minute. Are you trying to tell me that the painters missed this? I don't think so, Bethan.'

Bethan's freckles stood out sharply against his white face, the way they always do when he's frightened or angry.

'Well, *I* didn't do it,' he mumbled.

'Look at me, Bethan.'

'I didn't!'

'Well, it wasn't me,' I interjected, and Ray sidled out of the room. He doesn't like family arguments.

'I'll just get the paint,' he called, clumping down the stairs.

'This is very silly and childish behaviour,' Mum informed Bethan. 'And if you do it again, there'll be no TV for a month.'

'But I *didn't* do it!'

'Don't talk to me like that, thank you.'

'You *never* believe me! I *didn't* do it! Why should I?'

'Don't ask me, Bethan. Probably for the same reason that you wrapped the cat in toilet paper, and put all those silly things in the microwave oven.'

'That isn't fair!'

'Bethan,' said Mum, 'I'm not going to argue with you. One more time, and you won't be watching TV for a month.'

Well, I thought – that should do the trick. Bethan's a real TV addict, you see. And Mum hates television, so she's always happy to deprive us of it. I don't think she'd have it in the house, if it wasn't for Ray. Ray watches the news every night, religiously – he can't do without his news and current affairs.

Anyway, I wasn't surprised when Bethan stopped complaining about missed spots. Two days passed, and he didn't utter another word on the subject. I noticed that he was looking subdued, and distracted, and that he wasn't making his usual

10

blunt remarks and dumb jokes. (Maybe Mum would have noticed too, if she hadn't been so busy unpacking boxes.) In the end, I decided that some footballer must have been disqualified, or that Bethan had done something stupid at school. I mean, he was still eating like a vacuum cleaner and kicking his ball around the backyard. I didn't think that anything could be *really* wrong.

Not until he came to me one morning, with tears in his eyes, and begged me to look at his room.

Chapter Two

'**Why? What's happened?**' I asked.

'I have to show you,' he replied.

'Show me what?'

'Please,' he said.

Now, 'please' isn't a word that my brother uses very often, so I got a bit concerned. I looked at him closely, saw that he was seriously rattled, and stood up. I had been doing my homework, which was due on Monday, but some things are more important than homework.

I followed him into his room.

'There,' he said, pointing. 'And there, and there. See?'

I saw. There were more scribbled black lines

scattered around his white walls – about six of them. Some were too high up to read. One was on the back of his door: it said, *and his coasts were populous with fishermen*. Another was scrawled near the night-light.

I shook my head, slowly. 'Mum's going to kill you,' I said.

'But I didn't do it!' Bethan wailed. His voice cracked and began to wobble all over the place. 'I didn't, honestly, why doesn't anyone believe me? Al, I *don't know how they got here!*'

Frowning, I peered at him. He didn't sound like himself at all. Usually, when he starts protesting, his tone is very defensive. This time he just gave the impression of being upset. Upset and scared.

'Are you sure?' I pressed him.

'Yes! I didn't! It was someone else!'

'Who?'

'I don't know.'

It didn't seem likely. But when I looked at the writing again, it occurred to me that Bethan wouldn't have had the ability – let alone the patience – to write in such a precise, elegant way. Bethan's writing is big and round, with some letters squashed up and others stretched out. Not only that, but he needs lines under his letters if he wants them to stay straight and even.

The writing on the wall was straight and even without the help of lines.

13

'Do you think . . . I mean . . . it couldn't be Ray, could it?' I murmured, and we looked at each other.

'Ray?' said Bethan, in bewilderment.

'It can't be Mum. You saw how cross she was.'

'It can't be Ray. Why would Ray do it?'

'I don't know.'

Suddenly Bethan's face went red.

'It better not be you!' he cried. 'If it's you, I'm going to *kill* you!'

'It's not me.'

'Then who is it?'

I stepped back, and gazed around the room.

'Let's ask Mum,' I said.

So we went downstairs. It was Mum's turn to cook dinner, and she was making her risotto (which isn't one of my favourites), humming as she moved around her shiny, brand-new kitchen.

It seemed a pity to spoil her mood, but we didn't have any choice.

'Mum,' I said.

She looked up from the chopping board, and smiled. 'Yes, my darling?'

'Mum, there's something I've got to tell you. And you mustn't blame Bethan, because it's not his fault. Honestly. He didn't do it.'

Mum's smile faded. 'Didn't do what?' she asked.

I took a deep breath. Bethan and I exchanged a quick glance.

'There's more writing on his walls,' I explained, reluctantly, 'but it's not his writing.'

'I didn't want to tell you, because of the TV!' he blurted out. 'I don't like it, Mum, really I don't. Someone's coming into my bedroom!' His voice cracked again. 'It's *my* bedroom! No one else should be going in there.'

Mum laid down her knife. She fixed me with a very grave and serious look.

'Alethea,' she said, 'I want the truth, please. Do you know anything about this?'

'No,' I replied. 'Cross my heart.'

'Bethan? If you're lying, Bethan, I'm not going to forgive you for a very long time. Do you understand?'

'I didn't do it!' he squealed.

'He couldn't have done it, Mum,' I said, as something else occurred to me. 'Some of this stuff is written on the ceiling. How could he have written it on the ceiling? The ceilings in this house are so high.'

'Well . . .' She was starting to sound uncertain. 'We do have a ladder . . .'

'But how would Bethan get the ladder up those stairs? All by himself?'

We stared at him, Mum and I. He growled, 'Well, don't ask *me*.'

'Perhaps I'd better have a look,' said Mum. 'Bethan, why don't you go and get Ray? He's out

15

the back.' She wiped her hands on a tea towel, followed me down the hall and began to climb the stairs. 'You don't suppose this writing might be the old stuff?' she suggested. 'Soaking through the paint, for some reason? Maybe it was written in something that's reacting with the paint, as it dries.'

'I don't know,' I said. It was a reasonable explanation. But when we reached Bethan's room, and studied the writing, we began to have doubts. Surely, if the words had soaked through the paint, they wouldn't have been so clear and dark? Surely they would have been blurry?

'You don't think Bethan's lying, do you?' Mum asked me, in a low, worried voice. 'You don't think he's doing it himself?'

'No. I don't.'

'Not even to attract attention? I just – oh, dear. I hope this isn't a symptom of some kind of – I don't know – emotional problem.' Then she muttered something about therapy, and I was afraid that she might start mentioning alternative treatments like acupuncture again. (She's always suggesting that we have acupuncture, which I don't fancy at all. Injections are bad enough.)

'No, Mum,' I said firmly. 'That's not Bethan's writing. If only Bethan *could* write like that. It's grown-up writing.'

'That's true,' she admitted.

'In fact, it's more than grown-up – it's old-fash-
ioned. Like Granny's used to be. Oh!' And that's
when I realised. 'You know what it looks like?'
I gasped. 'It looks like the writing in that book
from under the stairs!'

Mum shot me a quick, startled glance. I could
see a hint of alarm in her expression.

'But it's probably a coincidence,' I added quickly.
I didn't like what I'd just said any more than Mum
did.

Then Ray appeared, with Bethan. They were
slightly out of breath.

'Ray, where did I put that book?' Mum asked.
'Do you remember? The old one, from under the
stairs?'

Blinking, Ray thought for a moment. Without
Ray, Mum would be losing things all the time. He's
very tidy and logical for an artist. In fact he doesn't
look like an artist at all. He has short hair and
glasses, and he irons his shirts (even his T-shirts),
and he's always cleaning the paint from under his
fingernails.

'I know I packed it,' Mum continued, 'but I can't
remember – did I put it in the bedroom bookcase
or in the bookcase downstairs?'

'Neither,' Ray replied, with decision. 'It's in that
cupboard in the studio, with the old magazines.'

So I was sent to fetch the book. Naturally, I studied the writing on its flyleaf all the way back to the bedroom, growing more and more uneasy as I did so. When I finally reached Mum, I couldn't get rid of the thing fast enough. Suddenly, I didn't want to be touching that mouldy old book.

'God,' said Mum, staring at it. 'God, Ray, would you check this out?'

'Lordy,' said Ray, adjusting his glasses. Bethan squeezed between them, and all three peered at the inscription on the flyleaf. Then they gazed at the wall. Then they fixed their eyes on the book again.

'Jeez,' said Bethan. He sounded both anxious and awestruck.

'It can't be the same,' Mum said plaintively. 'Not *exactly* the same.'

'I can't see much difference,' Ray replied. 'Compare the capital E in Eglantine with the one on the wall. There are a lot of ways you can write a capital E. These have the same loops. The same thickness of line.'

There was a long, long silence. No one wanted to come right out and say anything stupid. Not at first.

It was Bethan, of course, who finally couldn't resist.

'Do you think it's a ghost?' he squeaked.

'Oh, Bethan,' said Ray, and Mum remarked, in hollow tones, that there were no such things as ghosts – just concentrations of negative *chi* sometimes associated with past misfortune.

'If there's a ghost in this room,' Bethan went on, sulkily ignoring her, 'I don't want to sleep here.'

'It's highly unlikely, Bethan,' said Ray, in his gentlest voice. 'I'm sure there's another explanation.'

'Like what?' said my brother, sharply. He was really nervous, or he wouldn't have talked like that. Not to Ray. With Ray, he usually mumbles.

But Ray didn't take offence. He rarely does.

'Like maybe the squatters found that book,' he suggested. 'And maybe one of them was a bit – you know – odd, and copied the writing, and now the writing is soaking through the paint for some reason –'

'I'm still not sleeping in here,' Bethan said, at which point alarm bells began to ring for me.

'Well, he's not sleeping in *my* room!' I protested.

'A bit of writing isn't going to hurt you,' Ray sensibly pointed out, laying a hand on Bethan's shoulder.

Mum, however, was beginning to freak. 'Negative energy, Ray,' she said. 'The balance in here can't be good, surely?'

'Why not?'

'Well . . . I don't know, but –'

'I won't sleep in here,' Bethan declared, looking sick. 'It's giving me nightmares.'

That *really* made everyone sit up and take notice. Mum hissed through her teeth, and Ray asked, 'What kind of nightmares?'

I quickly pointed out that everyone had nightmares, I had them myself, and it didn't mean I had to move out of *my* room – but Mum shushed me.

Ray repeated his question.

'I dream that I'm choking,' Bethan mumbled. 'And then I wake up.'

'Just that?' said Ray. 'Nothing else?'

'I don't think so,' my brother replied, vaguely.

'And is that the only dream?'

'Yes,' Bethan admitted. 'But I've had it every night since we came. And,' he added, 'I've never had it before.'

Choking, I thought. Yuk. But I didn't let my sympathy get the better of me.

'We're each supposed to have our own bedroom,' I remarked. 'That's why we moved –'

'Oh, stop it, Alethea!' Mum snapped. She was worried, I guess, but she made me jump. 'Don't be so selfish!'

'*You* can sleep in this room, if you want to,' Bethan said to me, but Mum informed him that no one would be sleeping in his room that night.

He would be sharing my room until the mystery was solved – or until the writing stopped.

'And I don't want to hear one more word out of *you*,' she told me, 'or you'll be sleeping on the sofa.'

Which is how I lost my bedroom, almost before I'd had time to enjoy it. Boy, was I mad. It was so unfair! But I have to admit that, if I hadn't been so keen to get Bethan out of my room, the problem might never have been fixed. Because I might never have concentrated so hard on helping to solve it.

Chapter Three

That night, Mum did three things.

First of all, she phoned her friend Trish. Trish is a masseur, and even more of a hippy than Mum is. They're both into tofu, and yoga, and Feng Shui, but Trish has a much wider circle of vegetarian Buddhist astrologer friends. So it didn't surprise anybody when Trish said that she knew a woman who was a member of a group called PRISM (Paranormal Research Investigation Services and Monitoring). If Mum didn't mind, Trish said, she would ring this woman and see if they could all get together.

Mum replied that it was okay by her. The more help we had, the better it would be.

The second thing that Mum did was ask me to make a note of every word scribbled on Bethan's wall. She explained that it would help us to determine whether anything was added overnight. She also asked me to underline every word on the wall with a red pen, for the same reason.

So I got out my journal, and copied down the mysterious script. Ray had to bring a ladder before we could work out what was written on the ceiling: it was more strange stuff about kings and sailors and seaports, and it didn't make much sense. But I wrote it all down, and underlined it in red, and tried not to think about it again for a while (because I had to finish my homework).

I thought about it that night, though, when I was lying in bed. I thought about the writing, and about Eglantine Higgins, 1906. If there was a ghost in the house (which there probably wasn't, but if there was), then it was almost certainly the ghost of Eglantine Higgins. During the daytime, this hadn't worried me. After all, a bit of ghostly writing never did anyone any harm.

At night, however, I have to admit that it freaked me out. I didn't like the idea of Eglantine Higgins drifting around in the next room while Bethan and I were dead to the world. Perhaps that's why I didn't sleep very well. I didn't have bad dreams, but I kept waking up with a start.

I think I was half-expecting to find Eglantine Higgins hovering over my bed.

The third thing that Mum did, that night, was to take a long red hair from her head, stick one end of it to the bottom of Bethan's bedroom door, and stick the other end onto the base of his doorframe. She didn't tell us what she had done until the next morning. But she warned us, before we went to bed, that *no one* was to enter Bethan's room again before summoning her – and in the morning we found out why.

'Look,' she said, as we stood around Bethan's bedroom door in our dressing-gowns. 'See that hair?' We didn't, at first. She had to show it to us. 'That hair is unbroken. Which means that no one went through the door last night.'

We gazed at her in admiration.

'Wow, Mum,' Bethan exclaimed. 'That's really smart.'

'Good work, Mum.'

'Clever,' said Ray.

'So if there's anything new on the walls,' Mum went on (pointing out the obvious), 'whoever put it there didn't come through this door.'

'Unless you did it yourself,' I volunteered, and she made a face at me.

'Very funny,' she said.

'Well, it's true, isn't it?'

'Come on,' Ray interrupted. He sounded almost keen, though he doesn't usually get very excited about anything. 'Let's have a look.'

He pushed at the door. It creaked slowly on its hinges, like something out of a horror movie, revealing Bethan's light, bright, echoing room.

We saw the new writing at once. We couldn't have missed it: there were new lines everywhere – twenty-four, to be exact. (I counted them afterwards.)

'My God,' Mum breathed.

'This is so unbelievable.' I was the first one over the threshold. Timidly I advanced, clutching my journal and my blue fountain pen. *I am the proudest of my line* was new; it was inscribed at eye level, above the chest of drawers. I didn't recognise *I have the wherewithal to defend myself*, either. Quickly I opened my journal, and began to copy out these most recent messages.

Ray went to the window. He rattled it. The catch was firmly in place. 'No one could have come through here,' he declared. 'Not without leaving the catch open when they left.'

'What's happening, Ray?' Mum asked quietly.

'I don't know.'

'It doesn't seem possible, does it? I mean, it doesn't make any sense unless – well, you know what I mean.'

'I'm sure there's some chemical explanation,' he replied – but not with any conviction, I thought.

Bethan asked when 'that ghost woman' was coming.

'I'm not sure yet,' said Mum. 'Trish has to ring me.'

'Well, it had better be soon,' Bethan grouched, with a wary, sidelong glance at the walls. 'Because I want my bedroom back.'

Happily for all of us, Trish called Mum soon afterwards, bearing good news. The PRISM woman (whose name was Sylvia Klineberg) would be visiting us that very evening. Sylvia had suggested half past eight, so if Mum had no objections, Trish would ring Sylvia back and confirm the arrangements.

Mum had no objections.

'Come to dinner, won't you?' she pleaded with Trish. 'Early, at six. Then we can be finished and cleaned up by the time she appears.'

I hate it when Trish comes to dinner, because she eats macrobiotic food – which is rice and not much else. It's a bit bland. It also has a bad influence on Mum, who always starts talking about black bread and herbal teas and grinding her own grain. Personally, I like the food that she cooks for us now (except the risotto). I'd much rather have mashed potato and lamb cutlets than soy-and-birdseed rissoles.

26

Fortunately, however, at this particular dinner there were more exciting things to talk about than macrobiotic food.

'It seems to me,' said Trish, after much thought, 'that your house must be sitting on the intersection of a lot of ley lines.' When asked what ley lines might be, she explained that they were lines of energy, or life force, flowing over the earth. 'Ley lines connect all the world's sacred sites,' she assured us. 'And those points where ley energy paths converge are always prone to strange manifestations, because of the energy surges.'

'Too much earth energy,' Mum interjected, and Trish agreed that there was, indeed, a risk of imbalance.

'What kind of sacred sites are you talking about?' I asked, whereupon Trish began to reel off a list of them: churches, temples, stone circles, holy wells, burial grounds . . .

'Burial grounds!' Bethan exclaimed, his mouth full of food. 'Oh, no. You don't think this house was built on an Aboriginal burial ground, do you?'

Bits of rice sprayed all over the table as he spoke. Politely, Trish ignored them – or perhaps she didn't see them. She's a vague sort of person when it comes to things like electricity bills and table manners. Though she can be quite sharp about people's feelings.

27

She looks a little like a ghost herself, with her pale, skinny face and floating hair and layers of drifting shawls and scarves and Indian cotton skirts.

'I don't think it's likely, Bethan,' she responded, with the utmost sincerity.

'In America, haunted houses are always sitting on top of Indian burial grounds,' Bethan went on, in a glum voice. Mum said something about dispersing the negative energy — with wind-chimes, perhaps? At least they would moderate the *chi* flow where different energies converged.

'I don't know,' Trish replied. 'Perhaps you shouldn't start moderating energy flows until Sylvia takes a look at the place. She's had a lot to do with manifestations like this. She may help you to identify the problem.'

'How?' Ray inquired, and Trish said that she wasn't sure, exactly. She didn't know Sylvia very well. Sylvia was a naturopath who had treated Trish's friend, Alice. In her spare time, Sylvia went about investigating reports of paranormal activity for PRISM, which was a large organisation based in Adelaide. Trish had no idea what a paranormal investigator actually did.

'But I'm sure it will be very interesting,' she added brightly, and I could see that she had high hopes. Perhaps she was expecting that we'd all

28

have to sit in the dark, holding hands and waiting for the spirits of the dear departed to communicate with us. I was expecting much the same thing myself.

As it turned out, we had the wrong idea entirely. When Sylvia knocked at the door and we went to open it, we were all very surprised at how *normal* she looked. There was no fluttering black cloak. No crystal ball. She had short grey hair, and neat pearl earrings, and she wore a pale linen jacket over navy-blue trousers. She was carrying a green gym bag.

After she'd been invited into the kitchen for coffee, she took a notebook and a tape-recorder out of the gym bag before she sat down.

'Trish tells me that you've had unexplained writing on the walls of a bedroom,' she said, once everyone had been introduced to each other and her coffee had been poured. 'I guess you'd better tell me the story from the beginning. You've only just moved in, is that right?'

Mum said yes. She explained about the squatters. She described her improvements: the new kitchen, the new paint, the new window glass. She showed Sylvia the book from under the stairs, and – with many interjections from me and Bethan – related the strange tale of Bethan's bedroom. It all took a long time. Sylvia made notes as her tape-recorder whirred quietly away. She didn't say

29

much. She just listened, and I couldn't tell from her expression what she was thinking.

'Do you reckon it's a ghost?' Bethan finally asked her, and she gave a half-smile.

'That's what we have to establish,' she answered.

'If it *is* a ghost,' I said, 'it must be the ghost of Eglantine Higgins. Because it's got the same handwriting.'

'Perhaps,' Sylvia replied. She shut her notebook and turned off the tape-recorder. 'I suppose I'd better see the room, now,' she added, rising, whereupon we all trooped upstairs to look at Bethan's bedroom. The door was shut, of course; it had been shut all day. No one had been in there since nine o'clock that morning. When Ray clicked on the light switch, I couldn't see any evidence of further unexplained activity. Every word on the wall had been underlined in red, by me, at Mum's request.

'I think it only happens at night,' Mum remarked. 'Which is what you'd expect, really, isn't it? With a ghost.' She gave an unconvincing little laugh.

Sylvia didn't reply. She took out of her pocket a funny thing the size of a calculator, and began to pace the room with it.

Bethan asked her what it was.

'An electromagnetic field detector,' she replied.

Everyone – except Sylvia – exchanged glances.

'And what does it do?' Ray wanted to know.

'It identifies anomalies in electromagnetic readings.' Sylvia stopped, her gaze fixed firmly on her gadget. 'High volumes of electromagnetic activity are usually associated with poltergeist reports and so forth. Hmm.'

'What?' said Mum.

'Well . . . you do have a very high reading in here. Anything over point nine is a problem, and this room is registering point twelve.'

'Oh, dear,' said Mum.

Trish nudged her. 'You see?' Trish whispered. 'What did I tell you? Intersecting ley lines.'

'So there *is* a ghost in here?' Bethan inquired, but Sylvia wouldn't commit herself.

'Not necessarily.'

'Then what's happening?' Mum demanded. 'Who's doing this?'

Sylvia raised her eyes from her gadget. She surveyed us all in a way that made me feel uncomfortable.

'At the moment,' she said at last, slowly, 'we can't rule out a human agent.'

'What?' Mum cried, and Ray said, 'Who?'

'That is what we'll have to determine.'

'Well, it isn't me,' I announced. '*I* don't want Bethan in *my* room.'

'And it isn't me, either!' Bethan cried. 'I don't want to sleep with Alethea. I want my own room back!'

Sylvia looked at me long and hard. Then she looked at Bethan. Then she said, with a hint of apology, 'We have to rule out the possibility of human intervention before we can accept that any strange activity has a paranormal cause. It's standard procedure.'

'And then what?' asked Mum. 'If you rule out human intervention, what happens after that? How can you get rid of this thing?'

Sylvia blinked.

'Get rid of it?' she echoed.

'Yes. That's what you do, isn't it? You're a kind of ghost-buster, aren't you?'

'Well . . . no,' said Sylvia. 'Actually, I'm not.'

'You're not?'

'My job is to identify what the problem is – if it's paranormal or not. If it is, and you want it stopped, well . . . we can make some suggestions –'

'Like what?' Mum sounded quite cross, and Ray put a hand on her shoulder.

Sylvia watched them both cautiously. 'It depends on what you have here,' she said at last. 'And what your religious beliefs might be. You may want to talk to Laurie, in fact – he's our president. He may be able to help you. But really, nothing can be done until we establish exactly what it is we're dealing with.'

She went on to explain that, if the mystery was to be solved, she and some of the other investigators would have to spend at least one night in Bethan's bedroom, with their equipment. Would Mum object to that? Mum said no, she supposed not, since Bethan wouldn't be sleeping in there anyway. When was Sylvia planning to return?

'Oh, I'll have to get back to you,' Sylvia replied. 'As soon as possible. This is a very interesting case. I'm grateful that you brought it to our attention.'

And that was that. After peering at the ghostly handwriting one last time, Sylvia moved out of the bedroom briskly, her heels clicking on the floor.

I have to admit, it was a bit of a let-down. We had all been expecting her visit to be more dramatic.

'So I take it that my son shouldn't be sleeping in his room?' Mum inquired, as Sylvia said goodbye on the doorstep. 'I mean, with all that electro-magnetic activity?'

'It's entirely up to you,' Sylvia responded. 'A microwave oven registers sixty-five when it's switched off.'

'I won't have one of those things in the house,' said Mum, and Trish asked, 'What about wind-chimes? Would they moderate the negative energy?'

Sylvia raised her eyebrows. 'I'm not sure,' she said cautiously. 'But anything's worth a try.' Turning back to Mum, she added, 'If I were you, Judy, I would scatter some talcum powder on the floor of that room. It's a way of ruling out human intervention. We often use it ourselves.'

Then, after promising to call Mum as soon as possible, she disappeared into the shadows.

Chapter Four

Mum scattered talcum powder over the floor of Bethan's room before she went to bed that night. The next morning, the powder lay undisturbed, but the walls were covered in so many new lines of script that it took me an hour to copy them all down.

The copying took place after school, naturally. I didn't have time to do it in the morning. Besides, Mum didn't want me trudging around Bethan's room before she'd vacuumed up the talcum powder. So it wasn't until Monday evening that I made my interesting discovery about the text on the walls . . .

Before that happened, however, I spoke to the

school librarian. I'd been thinking about our family's problem all morning, off and on. (I usually finish my work long before everyone else does, and have to sit around waiting as a result. That's why I have so much time to think.) It seemed to me that we weren't going to get much help from PRISM – not until Sylvia was convinced that we actually had a ghost in the house. Weeks might pass, I thought, before anyone tried to stop the ghost from writing on our walls. And I didn't want to wait that long for sole custody of my bedroom.

I decided to do a bit of research. Instead of joining my friend Michelle in the playground, at lunchtime, I went to the school library, collected a stack of books about ghosts, and sat down to work out why ghosts haunt houses. After a lot of reading, I came to the following conclusion. Ghosts – if they exist – are tricky, unreliable things that don't respond well to being told what to do. Nevertheless, some of them need help. Some of them are only drifting about because their killers have gone unpunished, or because their earthly remains haven't been given a decent burial.

I wondered what could possibly have been troubling Eglantine Higgins. She couldn't have been buried under the house, because the house had been built in 1886, and Eglantine had been alive twenty years later. Had she died *in* the house, perhaps? Had someone killed her in it? That was a nasty thought, but it had to be faced.

I asked Mrs Procter, the librarian, how you could find out who had been living in your house a hundred years ago.

'Well,' she said, after some hesitation, 'that might be a bit difficult. Is this your new house, Alethea?'

'Yes.'

'Why do you want to know?'

I had no intention of telling her the truth. I was already having a hard enough time convincing people that I wasn't a weirdo – the last thing I needed was a reputation for seeing ghosts.

'Just some things we found,' I replied vaguely. 'A book and . . . other stuff.'

'I see.' She thought for a moment. I like Mrs Procter, because she always takes me seriously. She's very intelligent, too, and knows a lot about books. (I'm a favourite of hers, because I actually read them.) 'You might ask your neighbours,' she finally suggested. 'Sometimes people have been living in one place for a long while, and know things about the neighbourhood.'

I grunted. Our new neighbours weren't very friendly. On one side lived a big sloppy lady who spent all her time in front of the television, when she wasn't on the phone complaining to Mum about the noise of our renovations. On the other side lived a well-dressed young couple with an expensive car, who were hardly ever home. The big sloppy lady wouldn't talk to us any more. The young couple were never available.

'I don't think our neighbours would be much help,' I said.

'Of course, if you wanted to find out who *owned* the house a hundred years ago, you could check the title deeds,' Mrs Procter remarked. 'When your mother bought the house, her lawyer would have done a historical search, and had a copy made of the old title deeds. Title deeds show the names of all the past owners, and tell you when they bought the house. That might be useful – although just because a person owned a house, it doesn't mean that they lived there.'

Or died there, I thought. Then something else occurred to me.

'How do you find out where and when somebody died?' I asked. 'If it happened about a hundred years ago, say?'

Mrs Procter fixed me with a curious look.

'There's a name in the book we found under the stairs,' I added hastily. 'I want to find out if the person who owned the book lived in the house. And whether she's still alive.'

'I see,' said Mrs Procter. 'Well, you can check with the Registry of Births, Deaths and Marriages. There's one in every state. They keep records of death certificates.'

'Where's the New South Wales one?' I inquired, wondering doubtfully how I might persuade Mum to take me there. But Mrs Procter assured me that, like most other government bodies, the Registry would have its own internet site. I would simply have to log on.

'They do have rules about privacy,' she continued, 'but I don't think rules like that would apply to people who died a long time ago, or no one would ever be able to trace their family trees. Anyway, you should give it a try. Can't do any harm, can it?'

'No,' I said. But then the bell rang, and I had to put off looking at the Births, Deaths and Marriages site until the next day.

We don't have the internet at home, you see. Mum doesn't really trust it, for some reason – she says it's too expensive. She doesn't even like computers very much, despite the fact that she works in a bank. So I have to use a school computer, or one at the local library. It's very annoying. The school computers are nearly always hidden behind a crowd of boys who ignore you when you say that you've booked a session for an hour, and would they please move? As for the library computers, they're usually broken.

But that's neither here nor there. I was telling you about Monday. On Monday afternoon, I came home from school to find Mum vacuuming up the talcum powder in Bethan's room, and I told her what Mrs Procter had said about title deeds, and asked her where ours were.

'I don't have all those papers,' she replied without much enthusiasm. 'The solicitor has them.'

'Could you call the solictor?'

'I suppose so.'

'If we don't do *something*,' I declared, 'we'll *never* get rid of this stupid writing.'

'I'll call the solicitor when I finish the vacuuming,' Mum promised. And she did, too. And he said that he would send over a copy of the old title deeds as soon as he could.

So that was my first job done. My second job was to record and underline all the new lines of text on Bethan's bedroom wall, which, as I said earlier, took me an hour because there were so many. But as I copied them into my journal, I noticed something. To begin with, I noticed a name: Emilie. For the first time, a name had been used. *"Emilie is a good child* was written on the back of the door, and it was a sentence that caught my attention, not only because of the name, but

40

because of the opening quotation marks. Quotation marks mean that somebody's speaking. What's
more, you can't have one set of quotation marks at
the beginning of a line of speech without another
set closing the same passage. So I looked around
for more quotation marks, and found them – three
sets of them, widely scattered, all brand new – and
thought, I wonder if these quotation marks match
up, somehow? I wonder who's speaking?

That's when I settled down with my journal, and
began to piece all the lines of text together. It was
just like doing a jigsaw puzzle. With a jigsaw
puzzle, you always look for the corner pieces first,
and attach other pieces to them. With this funny
collection of stray sentences and phrases, I used
the quotation marks as my corner pieces. I also
used the name Emilie, which I tried to match up
with all the female references that were starting to
appear. (*My great crown would crush her smooth brow*,
for example.) It wasn't easy. But I made it easier by
cutting out every separate line of text – again, just
like a jigsaw puzzle. (I love solving puzzles.) Then
I arranged the pieces and rearranged the pieces,
and by dinner time I was pretty much convinced of
one thing.

Though the lines had been written all over the
place, they did fit together. They fitted together
into a story. It was even possible that they had

been written on the wall in order, and we hadn't noticed because we had spotted later lines before earlier ones.

Amazing? *I* thought so. Of course, I didn't have everything worked out by dinner time. There were more than sixty strips of paper to join up, and I had homework to do. But when I sat down at the kitchen table, I was able to inform everyone that the ghost upstairs was trying to tell us something, and that she wasn't finished yet.

Three heads turned.

'What do you mean, tell us something?' said Mum. 'What gives you that idea?'

'I've been putting all the sentences together,' was my response. 'They do make sense, when they're not scattered all over the walls. I think the ghost has been writing them out in the proper order, too, because the first few nights she was talking about a king and his kingdom, but last night the king started talking about a daughter. Emilie.'

'Wait – wait a second.' Ray lifted his hand. 'You're saying that the writing upstairs can actually be joined together? Into a composition of some kind?'

'Yes,' I said patiently. 'That's what I've been doing. Cutting out the lines and sticking them together with sticky tape. Like a puzzle.'

'What does it say?' Mum demanded. 'Is it some kind of message?'

'I don't know.' I thought about the little strips of paper spread over my bedroom floor. 'Maybe. It's about a white-bearded king, with mines, and sea ports, and a good navy, and a daughter but no son. The daughter's name is Emilie.'

'It sounds like a fairytale,' Bethan offered.

'Yes,' I replied. 'It does. That's just the way it sounds. That's just the way it's written.'

'But it might be a piece of history,' Ray mused. 'What king had a daughter called Emilie? Can anyone remember?'

Mum, however, wasn't interested in history. 'You said something about its not being finished,' she interrupted, fixing me with an anxious gaze. 'How can you possibly tell?'

'Well – I don't know. It doesn't *feel* finished.' I tried to work out why. 'Nothing's happened yet. I think the king wants an heir.'

'We should have a look at what you've done,' Ray said, 'and see what we think about it.'

'Do you reckon the writing'll stop when the story *is* finished?' asked Bethan, whereupon we all looked at each other.

I had to admit, it was a smart thing to say.

After a pause, Ray remarked, 'I wonder. That would solve the problem, wouldn't it?'

'As long as it's not a three-thousand-page novel,' Mum said. 'We'll be waiting years, if that's the case.'

'If that *is* the case, then we'll have to move out,' Ray declared. 'We can't live in a house that has a ghost permanently installed in one of the upstairs bedrooms.'

'Oh, but *Ray*,' Mum protested, 'think of the *expense*! Agents' fees and stamp duty –'

'I know, I know.'

'And all the work I've put into *this* house!' Mum wailed. 'I couldn't go through it all again.'

'I know,' said Ray, placing a hand on Mum's. 'It's all right. I'm sure we'll sort it out.'

Then Bethan asked, in a worried voice, whether the story on his bedroom wall contained any blood and guts. Anyone choking? Anyone suffocating? I knew just what he was getting at, and so did Mum. She said, 'The daughter's name in the story is Emilie, not Eglantine.'

'But they both start with E,' I pointed out. 'Maybe Emilie was Eglantine's second name. Or maybe Emilie stands for Eglantine. Maybe she *is* telling us what happened to her.' I started to get excited. 'Maybe she's disguising it as a fairytale, but it's really true! Maybe someone killed her, and she's trying to tell us how! Maybe that's why she's haunting us –'

'Maybe we ought to wait until PRISM has established if we *are* being haunted,' Ray broke in, firmly. At which point the phone rang, and Mum went to answer it.

It was Sylvia, calling to inquire about the type of paint used on Bethan's bedroom wall. She mentioned that she was consulting a chemical engineer about the possibility of substances reacting to other substances. There was a chance that the old writing was soaking through the paint, she said. Whatever she found out, she would call us again.

When she rang off, I grumbled, 'You see? She doesn't believe us.'

'She has to rule out every logical explanation,' said Ray.

'And meanwhile, Bethan's been kicked out of his own bedroom.' I was very cross. 'We should hire an exorcist, or something.'

But no one listened to me.

Chapter Five

I'd better explain about exorcists. Exorcists are people who perform exorcisms, and exorcisms are one way of driving out evil spirits. I'd learned about exorcisms when I was doing my research in the school library. I'd also learned that Catholic priests sometimes perform exorcisms, and I was wondering if Mum should call the local Catholic church when my friend Michelle discouraged me from suggesting it. But that was on Wednesday, and I haven't told you what happened on Tuesday, yet.

On Tuesday morning, I went straight into Bethan's bedroom as soon as I woke up. There, I found the walls and ceiling covered with so many new lines of text that very few blank spaces remained. One new line had even been written across an old one. It was obvious that very soon the room would be returned to its former state, almost black with unreadable scribblings. Bethan, when he saw this, was hugely depressed.

'Maybe it only stops when the room's totally black,' he moaned. 'Maybe the ghost just hates white paint.'

'That's possible,' I conceded. 'I wonder what would happen if Ray painted the room black?'

'But I don't want a black room!' Bethan said crossly. 'Black walls are for wankers!'

'Not necessarily,' I replied. I had to agree, however, that a black room would be pretty depressing. Even I didn't like the idea of sleeping in a black room. And I'm the sort of person who fills up her bedroom with animal skulls, a three-dimensional model of the inside of the human ear (bought at a garage sale) and portraits of dead kings (King Henry VII of England is my favourite).

'This is so annoying,' my brother continued. 'I hate this.'

'Are you still having those dreams?'

'No.'

'Then I don't see what you're complaining about.'

'I'm complaining because I don't have a room of my own!'

47

'Well,' I said witheringly, 'neither do I. And you don't hear *me* complaining.'

After that, we trudged down to breakfast and went to school. Actually, I did sympathise with Bethan. I even let him have the last pancake that morning. But when I got to school I began to regret my generosity, because by the time recess rolled around, it had become glaringly obvious that Bethan had been shooting his mouth off about having a ghost in the house.

First Malcolm Morling approached me and made stupid 'ooing' sounds as he fluttered his hands. Then, a little later, Amy Driscoll pranced up with her friend Zoe, and giggled, and nudged Zoe, and finally asked if it was true – was my house really haunted? When I told her 'No', she and Zoe exchanged glances, before exploding into another gust of giggles and scampering away.

By the time Jesse Gerangelos had called me a 'loony-tune', I was aware that rumours had been spreading. And I was very cross with Bethan. (It's no good getting cross with kids like Malcolm or Zoe; your best defence is to ignore them.) Though I had never actually *asked* Bethan to keep quiet about Eglantine, I had sort of assumed that she was a family secret. Why on earth would you make yourself a target for kids like Malcolm Morling? Most people don't believe in ghosts, you see, and laugh at people who do. Not only do they laugh – they make stupid ghost noises, and drape their jumpers over their heads, and generally make pests of themselves. A lot of the dumber kids at school already thought that I was odd, because I happen to like reading history books, and buying 'brain-teaser' magazines, and watching ants in the playground. (You'd think I was eating the ants, the way they carry on.) The last thing I needed was yet another reason for them to laugh at me.

I resolved to have a sharp word with my brother when we got home that afternoon.

At lunchtime I took refuge in the library, where I logged on to the website for the Registry of Births, Deaths and Marriages. I had to poke around a bit, but at last I found a link that told me exactly what I wanted to know. First of all, I typed out Eglantine's full name. Then I chose a ten-year period for a search of the Registry Index. The program can only search ten years at a time, you see, and I chose the years 1906 to 1916 – because I knew that Eglantine had been alive in 1906.

Within seconds, I was given the information that Eglantine Higgins, born in 1890, had died in 1907. I was disappointed that she had died in some totally unfamiliar place. But when I consulted Mrs Procter, the place turned out to be not a town or a suburb but a shire – our shire. So *that* was all right.

Eglantine Higgins had died in our shire, in 1907, at the age of seventeen.

Unfortunately, the website couldn't tell me how she had died. For that, it was clear, I would have to order a 'Family History Certificate'. Family History Certificates were copies of old death certificates, and they cost $20 each if you had a registration number. I did have a registration number (it had been given to me along with information about Eglantine's death), but I didn't have a credit card. To order a certificate over the net, you had to enter your credit card details.

That night, over dinner, I tackled Mum and Ray about our need for a Family History Certificate.

'It will tell us how Eglantine died,' I informed them. 'There was a sample certificate on the website, and it told you everything. Cause of death. Date and place of death. Where and when buried.'

'But why do we need to know these things?' Mum asked fretfully. (She'd had a bad day at work.)

'Because it'll help us to understand why the ghost is here! What if she was murdered in this house? What if her body was buried out in the backyard somewhere, and never found?'

'Would there be a death certificate if her body was never found?' asked Ray.

'I don't know. And we'll *never* know if we don't get a certificate.'

'Twenty dollars,' Mum sighed. 'That's a lot of money, Al.'

'I'll pay it,' Ray declared. He looked around the table. 'I'd be interested to see what it says. I'll log on tomorrow, and order one myself. What's the name of the website, Allie?'

I gave it to him. (It was www.bdm.nsw.gov.au.) Then I thanked him, and finished my ice-cream, and went upstairs to look at the latest instalment of Eglantine's fairytale. I've already said that she had been very busy, the previous night. It took me an hour and a half to underline and copy out all the new lines of text. But putting it together was easier, this time, because most of the second half seemed to be a description of Princess Emilie. First, there was a bit about an orphaned fisherman's son who had joined the navy of the white-bearded king. His name was Osric and, after fighting well in a couple of great battles, he had been made an officer and a count. Of course, he soon fell in love with Princess Emilie. It was love at first sight, because Princess Emilie was so beautiful. Her eyes were blue, her eyebrows black, her teeth small and pure. Her hair was brown and abundant, her mouth full-lipped and rosy. Even her upper lip was carefully described as *finely chiselled, with a thousand*

51

haughty contractions lurking in its ordinary quiet curve (whatever that was supposed to mean!). There was stuff about the strength of her jaw, the oval of her lower face, and the *severely intellectual character of her classic forehead*. It went on and on. After a while, the words got so long and complicated that I had to go to Mum for help. We spent three quarters of an hour putting together a sentence that had a hundred words in it!

In case you're interested, the sentence was: *When other moods possessed her, when the sultry and feverous heats of summer and the breath of too-rich flowers were upon her, when her blood was stirred by the bounding of her mettled horse, when old tales of adventurous love were ringing in her ears, and moonlight and heart-reaching songs were around her, then her breast heaved high and sank low with pulses of pleasure yet slumbering but ready to awake; her eyes swam with lustrous consciousness, and hung upon all beautiful sights with long gazes of langour so subtle that any lightest touch might quicken it to passionate ardour.*

I hope that makes sense to *you*, because it doesn't to me.

There was even more stuff like this on the walls the next morning, though of course I didn't read it until I got home from school. Mum said it was 'typically Victorian'. Michelle, when I showed her the text, said that it reminded her of poetry. She said that she had once read a poem that sounded a bit like it, and that she would ask her mother what the name of the poem was.

Michelle is my best friend. She has a French grandmother, so she isn't embarrassed about reading poetry. In fact she isn't embarrassed about anything much: she's elegant, and confident, and she gets high marks in geometry and maths. On Wednesday, she heard from Amy Driscoll that I was living in a haunted house. When she asked me about it, and I growled at her, she seemed surprised.

'Why are you so prickly?' she wanted to know. 'I was only interested.'

'Sorry,' I said. 'But everyone's been joking about me.'

'Have they? I haven't heard them.'

'Malcolm Morling thinks I'm crazy.'

'That's because he's crazy himself.'

'I don't want to talk about it. Honestly.'

But Michelle dragged it out of me – I don't know how. She can be very persuasive. I told her about the writing, and about Sylvia Klineberg, and about Eglantine Higgins. I told her about the book from under the stairs, and Eglantine's fairytale. By the time I had finished, Michelle was more excited than I'd ever seen her.

'You must show it to me,' she begged. 'This afternoon!'

'Well . . . I don't know . . .'

'*Please*, Allie!'

In the end, I agreed. Michelle doesn't live far from my house, so it was easy to arrange. She walked home with me from the bus stop, and we went straight upstairs to Bethan's bedroom. Here there was something new – a dangling set of silvery windchimes. It hung from the light fitting.

'Mum must have put it there,' I remarked, as we gazed up at the tinkling arrangement of miniature pipes. 'She thinks that windchimes might help.'

'How?'

'I don't know. Something about dispersing bad energy.'

'They're not going to work very well if you keep the door and window shut.'

'Maybe they don't have to make a noise. Maybe they just have to be there.' I mentioned my idea about an exorcist. 'An exorcist,' I said, 'would be better than windchimes. Exorcists drive out evil spirits. I read it in a book.'

But Michelle looked grave.

'What makes you think this spirit is evil?' she inquired.

'Well, it's keeping Bethan out of his bedroom, isn't it? I call that evil.'

'I don't know,' said Michelle, shaking her head. 'Exorcists – I've heard about exorcists. A film was made about them. It's my cousin's favourite film, and the ghost in this house doesn't sound like the evil spirit in that film.'

'Why? What happened in the film?'

'My cousin told me.' Michelle's voice became solemn. 'It was about a demon, not a ghost, and it killed people. It threw them out windows, and twisted their heads around and vomited green slime, and cracked ceilings, and pushed over furniture, and slammed doors, and made people speak in strange, spooky voices. And two priests died trying to exorcise it.'

'Oh,' I said. That made me think. I looked around the pale, quiet, sunny room. 'Perhaps we don't really need an exorcist.'

Michelle agreed. Then she had to go home, so I said goodbye, and started to copy down the new lines of text. There were ninety-four of them. When I pieced them together, I discovered that Count Osric had declared his love to Princess Emilie. In response, Princess Emilie blushed and trembled, and he pressed his lips to her white hand before they were interrupted.

From that time on, whenever his ship came into port, she would send a page to look for Count Osric. Once, she even disguised herself as a page, and saw Osric with her own eyes, from a distance. But suddenly the white-bearded king decided that his daughter should be married to the son of another great king, *whose realm adjoined his own beyond the mountains, and who had been evermore a rival*. The other great king was sent a message, which said, *Make with me now this treaty of alliance, and send hither thy son. By my faith, I will give him my daughter to wife*.

I was beginning to have a bad feeling about the end of this fairytale.

'What happened to Romeo and Juliet?' I asked Mum that night. 'They killed themelves, didn't they?'

'Yes.'

'Why?'

'Because their families were enemies, and they loved each other.'

'Was it based on a true story?'

'No,' Mum said, and hesitated. 'At least,' she added doubtfully, 'I don't think so. It was a play. By William Shakespeare.'

'I know *that*,' I replied, and wondered if Eglantine might have killed herself. For love, like Juliet. Was that possible?

Then Sylvia rang. She wanted to know if she could come around on Friday night, with another investigator, and stay over in Bethan's bedroom. They wouldn't be any trouble, she promised. We wouldn't even know they were there.

Mum agreed, of course. What else could she do? She was beginning to get desperate.

Chapter Six

The windchimes didn't work.

By Friday evening, there was so much writing on the wall that I had begun to lose track of the story. From what I *could* piece together, I learned that a young prince had been sent to marry Princess Emilie, and everyone in the kingdom was preparing for the nuptials (that means wedding, according to Mum). Emilie wept and prayed, but the king stormed till he foamed at the mouth, for though he loved his daughter, he was also *truculent and high of mood*. Then Osric arranged a meeting with Emilie. I'm not sure how, because that bit was written over another bit, and impossible to read. But there was a long conversation strewn across the walls which involved Osric and Emilie, and a lot of 'thee's and 'thy's. For example:

"Emilie, I think you love me."

"And if I do, Osric – what then: is it strange? Have I not heard thy voice growing ever more musical for my hearing, than for other ears? Have I not felt thy questing glance, thy probing words, going deeper into my heart than any other words or glance have ever been? If I do love thee Osric, I cannot help it, – what then?"

After this, everything was a tangled mess, lines written over lines. I was able to make out *His eyes were full of hope and enterprise*, *My love is not an idle passion* and *There are retreats where we may hide deep enough away*. There was something about a drooping head and yielding mien – something else about a consenting word forever undoing the ties that bind. But I couldn't get all the words to join together.

It was annoying, I can tell you. And even more annoying was Sylvia's reaction, when she arrived with her fellow investigator on Friday night. But before I tell you about that, I should tell you about Friday afternoon. On Friday afternoon, I came home to discover that the copy of Mum's title deeds had arrived. Mum told me the news as soon as I walked in the door, and handed me a long piece of paper with a coat of arms at the top and a lot of typed words sitting above a series of scribbled-on stamps.

'Prescott-Marsh, of Burrough, Teens and Walgrove,' I read aloud, 'is now the proprietor of an Estate in Fee Simple, subject nonetheless to the reservations and conditions, if any, contained in the Grant hereinafter referred to . . .'

'Not that bit,' Mum interrupted. 'Down there.'

'Where?'

'That stamp. Each stamp is a new owner. You see? This mortgage here was discharged to Ernest George Higgins in March 1894.'

'Higgins!' I exclaimed.

'He was probably Eglantine's father. And look – the next owner bought the place in 1907. The year she died.'

I gasped.

'Ernest Higgins moved out,' Mum continued, 'the very year she died.'

'Because she died in his house!' I declared.

'Not necessarily.'

'But it makes sense, Mum. Why else would you move out of a perfectly good house? Because your daughter died in it, of course!'

'Because someone strangled her in my bedroom,' Bethan suddenly remarked. He had come in quietly, and was peeling a banana from the fruit bowl. 'That's probably what happened.'

'Maybe her *father* strangled her!' I added. 'Maybe he had to sell the house because he went to gaol.'

'Now, stop it,' said Mum, with a frown. 'You're being silly.'

'But, Mum, just think.' I myself was thinking – thinking hard. 'In the story, the white-bearded king wants his daughter to marry a man she's not in love with. Maybe the same thing happened here. Maybe it was like that TV series, "Nicholas Nickleby", where the father was bankrupt and wanted his daughter to marry a rich man, and she wouldn't because she was in love with someone else, so in this case he strangled her –'

'That's enough!' Mum snapped. 'You're being revolting and melodramatic. I don't want any more talk about stranglings in this house!'

But of course there *was* more talk about stranglings that night, because the two PRISM investigators came. Sylvia turned up in a neat pair of track-pants, a white woollen jumper and some very old running shoes. With her she brought a young guy named Richard Boyer, who was thin and pale and very keen. He had bright blue eyes behind steel-rimmed glasses, and a quick, breathless way of talking. He was some sort of computer expert.

When I told him about Eglantine, and Bethan told him about the choking nightmares, he suggested that Eglantine might have died, not because she was strangled, but because she had asthma.

'I get asthma,' he said, looking at Bethan. 'Did it feel as if someone had parked a truck on your chest?'

'No,' Bethan replied. 'It was as if someone was stuffing something down my throat.'

'Hmmm,' said Richard. Then he began to talk about other examples of ghostly writing on walls, including one called the Borley Rectory hoax that I'd read about at the library. He seemed very excited. He couldn't sit still but kept jumping up, again and again, and roaming around the kitchen before returning to his seat. The sight of Eglantine's book was almost too much for him; his hands trembled as he opened it.

'Fascinating,' he said. 'Fascinating. Tennyson's *Idylls of the King*. Is this the same text that's written on the bedroom walls?'

'No,' I replied. 'That book is poetry. The stuff upstairs – well, it isn't poetry.'

'Maybe we should destroy the book,' Ray suddenly remarked. He had been standing quietly near the fridge. 'Has anyone thought of that? Maybe the book contains some – I don't know – some essence or anchor that's keeping Eglantine in this house. Maybe we should burn the book.' As everyone turned to stare at him, he gave an embarrassed little smile. 'Well,' he finished, 'it's just a suggestion.'

'It's a good one,' I said.

But Sylvia would have none of it. '*I'll* take the book,' she declared. 'I'll take it out of the house, and we'll see if that makes any difference. I don't think it ought to be destroyed just yet. Not when it contains this sample of Eglantine's handwriting. Incidentally,' she added, 'we might have this hand-writing dated, if possible. By an expert.'

'But it was written in 1906,' I pointed out. 'It's already dated.'

'Of course,' she replied. 'The question is – are we sure it's the correct date?'

After a lot of thought, I finally realised what she was getting at. She was saying that Mum, or Ray – or someone else – might have forged Eglantine's name, to match the writing that they also might have put on the walls. (Human intervention, in other words.) But before I could point out, once again, that we didn't *want* any writing on the walls, Sylvia was shepherding Richard up to Bethan's bedroom.

'Oh, no,' she said, as she walked in. 'Oh, no, this is no good.'

'What do you mean?' Mum asked.

'There's so much writing. There are no blank spaces.'

'No,' Mum said patiently. 'That's what I was telling you. It's been getting worse and worse.'

'But there's too much. It will be impossible to monitor.'

'I beg your pardon?'

Richard explained that they had been intending to make a record of any paranormal activity in Bethan's bedroom using infra-red video cameras and time-lapse photography. They had been hoping to film at least one line of script appearing on a stretch of white wall.

'If we take a wide shot of *this*,' he said, gesturing, 'it will be difficult to see any new writing against the old. If it was clean, we wouldn't have any trouble.'

'We'll have to paint over it,' Sylvia declared. As everyone looked at her, she continued, 'Tomorrow, Richard. We'll get a can of white paint and you can paint over the walls. Not the ceiling – just the walls. Then we can start from scratch.'

'But we'll have to photograph everything first,' Richard insisted.

'Oh, of course. That goes without saying.'

'Uh – excuse me.' Mum sort of put up her hand, like a kid at school. 'You're going to *paint the room*, again?'

'If that's okay with you, Judy.'

'Well . . . I guess so.'

'Richard will do it, won't you, Richard?' Sylvia went on. 'I can't, tomorrow – I'm booked up until the evening. And that's when we'll be wanting to come back.'

'Will the paint be *dry*, by then?' Mum inquired doubtfully.

'Oh, I think so.'

'Unless you need two coats,' said Ray. 'You probably will.'

'We'll see what happens,' Sylvia remarked. Then she picked up her tape-recorder, and her infra-red camera, and her electromagnetic field detector, and went home.

Richard went too, though not before photographing every square centimetre of Bethan's bedroom. He spent about two hours doing that, and left at nine forty-five. The next day he returned at eight-thirty in the morning, with two cans of white paint, a drop-sheet, a camera, a paint-roller and a pair of overalls. He was very enthusiastic when he discovered that the walls were messier than ever.

'So it didn't work – taking the book away,' he said.

'No,' I replied. I hadn't bothered trying to copy out the new lines of text. They were impossible to read, you see.

Bethan and I watched Richard for a while as he took another roll of photographs. Then Bethan wandered away, and I started to help with the painting. It quickly became obvious that Richard needed a lot of help – more help than I could offer. He didn't seem to know much about painting.

'I borrowed all this equipment from my dad,' he admitted, after realising that he had forgotten to bring a tray for the paint-roller. Fortunately, Ray had one of those. He also had a ladder, and a bottle of mineral turpentine, and some paint-spattered old trousers.

By ten o'clock, Ray was working beside Richard while Mum went off to do the shopping. I helped clean the brushes and listened to Richard's stories. One was about a haunted post office, which somebody had turned into a guesthouse. Several visitors had reported going to bed, switching off the light, and feeling the weight of a person sitting beside them. When the light was switched on, however, there was no one else in the room.

Another story was about a house where the doors kept slamming, where ghostly footsteps were always being heard, and where the crockery in the kitchen kept rearranging itself. Close investigation revealed that draughts, rats and a naughty grandchild were responsible for these 'paranormal activities'.

'You have to keep an open mind,' Richard revealed. 'It's no good coming in with your own ideas about something. You have to set aside your beliefs before you walk through the door.'

'Do *you* believe in ghosts?' I asked, and he laughed a little.

'I'm not sure,' he said, 'honestly. I'd *like* to believe in them. I haven't seen anything so far that's really convinced me – but on the other hand, I've heard some pretty amazing stories from people I trust, level-headed people who don't lie about things like that.'

'How did you get involved in PRISM?' Ray wanted to know.

Richard told him that, about a year before, he had stumbled onto PRISM's website and had decided to join. This was only his second investigation. The first had been a case of faulty electrical wiring.

'Your case looks *much* more interesting,' he said. 'Especially if we can get something on film.'

'Can kids join PRISM?' Bethan inquired from the door. To my horror, I saw that he was with his friends Matthew and Jonah. So *that's* what he's been doing since he left, I thought: rounding up the neighbourhood!

Richard knitted his brows. 'I don't know,' he replied. 'I don't know of any kids who are members. But that's not to say it's against the rules.'

'Do you get paid?' asked Matthew, and Richard laughed again.

'No. It's a non-profit organisation.'

'If I was a ghost-buster, I'd ask them to pay me,'

Matthew declared, squinting down the barrel of his plastic gun. Then he roared off, taking the other two boys with him.

They came back, however, several times. They seemed fascinated by Richard Boyer – though not by the ghostly writing. If it had been up to them, our ghost would have been performing more impressive tricks. Walking around headless, maybe, or making the walls bleed. They were a bit bored by endless lines of small, neat script.

Even so, they brought some of their friends to have a look. By the end of the day, we'd had seven kids through the house, wanting to see the 'haunted room' with their own eyes. Matthew and Jonah brought their friends Thomas and Gabriel. Michelle brought her cousin Dommy. And a little kid named Jostein from across the street knocked on the door after lunch to ask if he could please meet 'Caspar the friendly ghost'. Don't ask me how *he* heard about Eglantine. Obviously the news was spreading like wildfire.

No wonder our local newspaper got hold of the story.

Chapter Seven

Actually, we didn't hear from the local paper until Wednesday – and several things happened before that.

First of all, Richard Boyer spent Saturday night in Bethan's room. Sylvia tried to do the same thing, but was driven out very quickly by the paint fumes, which gave her a headache. Though Ray had left the window open after finishing the second coat, the fumes were still pretty bad; Richard looked pale and sick the next morning. I found him in the kitchen, drinking coffee, when I came down to breakfast.

Mum was already wide awake, eating her home-made muesli.

'So how did it go?' I asked, and Richard blinked

at me. Then he took off his glasses and rubbed his eyes.

'Oh – ah – pretty good,' he said.

'Is there any new writing?'

Suddenly he perked up. 'Yes,' he replied. 'Yes, there is. I counted ten new lines.'

'Great!' I opened the fridge. 'Did you see who wrote it?'

'No.' Richard sounded crestfallen. 'I mean, I probably got it on film – certainly the talcum powder wasn't disturbed . . .'

'He fell asleep,' Mum supplied.

'Even if I'd been awake, I probably wouldn't have seen anything,' said Richard, a little defensively. 'It was too dark. That's why we had the infra-red set up.'

'Then why did you have to stay in there at all?' I wanted to know, dumping the milk on the table.

'Oh, I had to do that. I had to.' Richard straightened, and his voice became more breathless than ever. 'I dreamed that dream, for one thing. I dreamed that I was choking.'

Mum and I exchanged glances.

'It was incredible,' Richard continued, furiously scratching his scalp with both hands. 'Exactly like Bethan said. Not asthma – nothing like asthma. Not a pressure on the windpipe, either. It was as if something was being forced down my throat.'

'What?' asked Mum.

'I don't know. It was all dark. Of course,' he added ruefully, 'dreams don't mean much, in the circumstances. I was already thinking about Bethan's dream. My mind was probably responding to the power of suggestion.' Suddenly Richard leapt to his feet, and scurried out of the room. He seemed to have the jitters, and looked quite awful, all red-rimmed eyes and drawn, white face.

But he still seemed very enthusiastic about the possible results of his investigation. Before he packed up his equipment and left, he thanked Mum again and again for her hospitality. And he assured her that he would ring us as soon as he had anything at all to report.

As it happened, however, I was the first one with something to report. Because after Richard had gone, and I went up to Bethan's room, I discovered that Count Osric was begging Princess Emilie to run away with him. *Lady*, he said, *hast ever a trusty page in thy train?* When Emilie replied that she did have a trusty page, he urged her to disguise herself as her page's brother, and *go forth at night from the palace's northern gate.* Once through the gate, she was supposed to *traverse the city's great street* until a forest was at her left hand; then she was to enter a path that would appear, and follow it until her *dear foot* should press a cliff above the sea.

'I don't think those PRISM people are paying enough attention to the story,' I remarked to Mum, after informing her of these latest developments in Eglantine's fairytale. 'That Richard guy didn't say anything about it. But it must have *some* meaning, don't you think?'

Mum grunted. I soon learned that she was losing faith in PRISM's ability to help her, because that afternoon Trish came over and spent two hours discussing Bethan's bedroom with Mum. They decided that its *chi* must be all wrong. Mum wondered if she should hang a crystal over the window, or place a light in the 'seventh house' to counteract all the thunder energy. Trish began to talk about the Predecessor Law.

'I'd forgotten about it,' she said, 'until I read my books again. Basically, the overall vibration that remains in a space from those who lived there before you controls much of what's happening now. That's the Predecessor Law. And it's beyond anyone's ability to change the Predecessor Law by installing cures or studying the *bagua*.'

'Then what am I supposed to do?' Mum demanded. 'For heaven's sake, Trish –'

'It's all right. Calm down. There *is* a solution.' No doubt Trish began to describe what the solution was, but at that point I wandered away to look at a nature program on the television. So I missed

71

what she said, and as a result I was very surprised when I came home, on Monday afternoon, to find Mum and Trish in Bethan's room, performing a purification ceremony.

They were both dressed in white. Trish wore a long, fluttery white dress. Mum had dug up a pair of old tennis shorts, a white T-shirt and a pair of white socks. They were sitting on the floor, cross-legged, with their eyes closed, making a long, low, breathy noise that sounded a bit like 'suuuuu'.

'What are you doing?' I asked, and Mum frowned without opening her eyes.

'Go away, Allie,' she said.

'But what –'

'It's all right, Allie,' Trish murmured. 'You can watch from the door, as long as you're very, very quiet.'

At first I thought they must be meditating. Mum does that, every so often, though usually not in white clothes. But then Trish began to speak. Not to chant – to speak. Her voice was low and soothing.

'Thank you very much for your life,' she said. 'Whoever you are, whenever you lived in this house, I'm sure you left it more beautiful than it was when you arrived. Wherever you are now, we hope that you can be happy and at peace, and we'll try to help you. Don't worry about this house. We love it, and we'll care for it, so you don't have to

72

stay here any longer. We wish you well. Don't worry about us, either, because we will seek to be happy and healthy without your presence . . .'

She went on and on, for about ten minutes. Then she chanted one of her sutras, and Mum chanted one of *her* sutras, and when they finished, they clapped their hands sharply three times, in unison.

Only at that point did they open their eyes, and struggle to their feet with a great cracking of knee-joints.

'Do you think Eglantine is really worried about the house?' I began, but Mum shushed me again. She took a handful of sea-salt from a little silver dish beside her and began to scatter it over the floor.

'We'll leave that there for a day,' Trish announced. 'Then we'll sweep it up and scatter some fresh flowers, instead. Perhaps light a few candles.'

'What's the salt for?' I inquired.

'Salt is the densest ingredient that we use in everyday cooking,' Trish replied solemnly. 'It's one of the most important elements of *life*, and therefore stands in direct opposition to the spirit world. We want to encourage the *life force* in this room.'

'It's worth trying,' Mum added. 'If this doesn't work, we'll have to bring in a Feng Shui master, and that's going to cost money.'

She left the room, then, and Trish went with her; they were going to refresh themselves with some jasmine tea. I stayed. I looked around at the bright, empty room, and wondered if Eglantine was going to take any notice of a Chinese purification ritual. I worried that she wouldn't, because she hadn't been Chinese.

'Eglantine,' I said aloud, 'I'm really, really sorry about what happened to you.' I was, too. I was beginning to feel as if I knew her better, and the fact that she might have choked to death . . . well, I was finding it harder and harder to think about anything so awful. 'The thing is, though,' I went on, 'there's nothing we can do about it. Can't you see that? Can't you please go away and leave us alone? I bet *you* wouldn't have liked sharing a room with *your* little brother.'

A deep, dense silence answered my request. Dust-motes drifted through a shaft of sunlight.

If Eglantine had heard me, she wasn't the least bit interested.

I went and got my journal, so that I could copy down the twenty-eight new lines that had appeared on the walls the previous night. Count Osric was still relating to Princess Emilie his plan for her escape. *I will anchor my ship against the cliff,* he said. *A red light shall float at the masthead. I will come with a boat and bear thee away. Then, with the strong ship*

*we will go to another land — a summer-land, where we shall
be forever happy. Oh, fly with me, lady, or I die! Fly with
me, I pray thee by our love. I bid thee from all pains. I proffer
thee all delights!*

But Emilie was doubtful. When he implored her,
she begged him to *command her, rather* — for without
his command, she would not have the strength. So
he commanded her, and she obeyed.

Then night fell upon the kingdom of the white-
bearded king, bleak and dark and cold. The shrubs
were heavy with raindrops which lurked in the
hollows of the blossoms and the leaves. A cold
wind blew. Emilie *arrayed herself like a page*, and went
forth to meet her lover. She left the palace gate.
She traversed the crowded streets. She trembled
but did not faint. She had just passed the sentries
at the city gate, when the story stopped.

By this time, I have to admit, I was becoming
obsessed. I wanted to know what was going to
happen. So I wasn't as pleased as you might expect
when, the next morning, I found only one line
written on the walls. It said, *A wood was at her left.*

'Wow,' said Bethan. 'Just one line.'

'That's pretty good,' said Ray. 'That's better than
we've had since the very beginning.'

'Maybe the purification ceremony was the right
thing to do,' said Mum, sounding a little dazed.
We were all standing around in Bethan's bedroom,

staring at the lonely new line. *A wood was at her left.*

I thought, Emilie and her page must be about to reach the edge of the sea-cliff.

'Maybe I should perform the ceremony again,' Mum continued. 'One more time for luck, do you think?'

'What about the flowers?' I inquired. 'Weren't you supposed to wait for a day, and then scatter flowers and light candles?'

'I'll ask Trish,' said Mum. She did – that afternoon – and Trish told her on no account to disrupt the order of proceedings. First the salt had to be swept away, she instructed. Then the flowers had to be scattered and candles placed about the room, particularly in the seventh house. After two days, the room could be cleared. 'And if you're still getting the odd line of text,' Trish added, 'then you can go through the ritual once more. Just to reassure the spirit, and give it release. But I doubt you'll have any more trouble,' she concluded confidently.

She was wrong. On Wednesday morning, I found ten new lines.

This was after Mum had spent thirty-six dollars on flowers from the florist, and burned through a whole packet of kitchen candles.

She was very cross.

'All right,' she growled, glaring around Bethan's

bedroom. 'If that's how you want to play it, Miss Higgins, we'll do it the hard way!'

And she went downstairs to telephone the Feng Shui master.

Chapter Eight

For the next few days, our house was like a hotel, with people in and out of it all the time.

Firstly (as I mentioned before) a journalist from the local newspaper called us, and asked if she could come over the next day, and take some photos. Having heard that our house was haunted, she wanted to write a story. She seemed particularly interested in the fact that PRISM was involved.

It turned out that she'd been told about us while collecting information for a story about the local under-twelves soccer team (from one of the Bracco brothers, probably). Mum agreed to an interview – I don't know why. Possibly she liked the journalist, and couldn't say no. Certainly the poor journalist was very young and timid, and hard to turn down. Her name was Claire Hickey. She had a shy little voice, and lank blond hair, and she looked a bit like a white rabbit. Mum let her take a photograph of Bethan's room – with Bethan in it – and Bethan, needless to say, was thrilled. He's a real publicity hound.

After Claire had gone, I pointed out that newspaper stories about haunted houses were always stupid ones, poking fun at the whole idea of ghosts.

'Claire's not like that,' said Mum. 'She's a very polite, serious girl. She doesn't think we're silly.'

'She doesn't?'

'No. Not at all. She told me that her grandmother once saw a ghost. And she *promised* not to give out our address.' Mum hesitated, perhaps as she realised that journalists don't always keep their promises. 'Anyway,' she declared, 'this is her first job, poor little thing. Her wages are woeful. And she's so keen. I had to help her out.'

Claire visited us on Thursday afternoon. On Friday evening, the PRISM investigators returned. Richard had called Mum on Wednesday, to inform her that the result of Saturday night's investigation had been 'inconclusive'. His aperture settings had been wrong.

'Infra-red's a tricky thing,' he apologised, 'and

falling asleep didn't help. I'm really sorry. I've worked it all out now, though. I've been practising. Would you mind *very* much if we came one more time? Just once more, I promise. Because I really think you've got something, there.'

With a sigh, Mum said 'yes'. So on Friday evening we welcomed Richard and Sylvia into the house again, pointing out as we did so that Bethan's bedroom walls were already pretty well covered with text.

'That's all right,' said Sylvia. 'We'll manage. We've brought several cameras, so we'll focus each one on a different stretch of white space. Did you bring the coffee, Richard?'

'Yes. I brought the coffee.' Richard flashed Mum a grin. 'I'm not going to fall asleep *this* time,' he assured her.

'From what Richard tells me,' Sylvia continued, 'there does seem to be something very odd happening in that room. Hopefully, we'll find out what it is tonight. Oh!' She began to search through one of her bags. 'Here's that old book you gave me. According to Richard, taking it away didn't make any difference – is that right?'

'No,' said Ray. 'I told you we should have burned it. Maybe we should do that now –'

'Oh! No! Wait!'

Mum's shriek made us all jump; we were standing

in the kitchen, surrounded by PRISM technology, and Ray nearly dropped his coffee cup.

As we stared at Mum, she exclaimed, 'Wait! Wait! Give me that book!' She snatched it from Sylvia's hand, and waved it at us. 'Maybe we should *put it back*!' she cried. 'Maybe that's the whole problem. It was taken out from under the stairs – maybe it ought to be returned!'

Everyone exchanged glances.

'Maybe moving that book started this whole thing in the first place!' Mum finished, triumphantly. But Ray shook his head.

'That can't be right,' he objected. 'Remember what that room looked like when we first bought the place? And the book was still under the stairs *then*.'

Mum's face fell. 'Oh,' she said. 'Yes. Of course.'

'I still say we should burn it,' Ray said firmly. 'It can't hurt.'

'It might,' I pointed out. 'It might make Eglantine mad. Madder than she is now, I mean. It's her book, after all.'

Ray began to laugh, hopelessly. 'I can't believe that we're having a serious discussion about a ghost's state of mind,' he groaned. 'Sometimes I feel like I've gone insane.'

'It's all right.' Sylvia did her best to comfort him. 'I know it's hard, but it'll sort itself out. Just don't burn the book, if you please. Not yet. Not until we have a record of this nocturnal activity, at the very least. Now – where's my double adaptor?'

She and Richard were all settled in upstairs by ten o'clock. They sat near the door, one on either side (in case they had to go to the toilet), clutching their torches and their thermos flasks. The floor was covered with talcum powder. Red lights blinked and tape-recorders whirred as Mum quietly closed the door on them. She said she felt as if she were shutting a hatch on a deep-sea diving capsule, or a space-shuttle cockpit. She giggled nervously as she wondered, aloud, if we would ever see them again.

I was quite prepared for a noisy night, full of startled screams and frantic curses. In fact I didn't expect to sleep very well. But I did, and was awakened the next morning by the sound of excited whispering in the hall. Because it wasn't even six o'clock – and because I *never* get up before seven on Saturdays, unless I absolutely have to – I turned over and went back to sleep. So I missed the two investigators, who were gone by seven.

They left a note on the kitchen table, thanking Mum for her patience and promising to ring soon because their results looked *very promising*.

As it turned out, they didn't call for another three days. When they did, it was to inform us that they had captured something on film. One of the cameras had picked up an image of four black words appearing on a stretch of white wall. It was incredible. Remarkable. But it did raise a question.

'The words weren't written out one by one, across the wall,' Sylvia explained to Mum. (I was listening on the extension.) 'They seemed to emerge from it slowly. They all started off very faint and became darker and darker, as if they were soaking through the paint. That's why,' she added, 'we can't yet rule out some kind of chemical reaction.'

'But the lines are appearing *in order*,' Mum objected. 'They're telling a *story*. How can they be part of a chemical reaction if they're telling a story?'

'That's what we have to find out. That's why we're going to consult a chemical engineer and get back to you. The film has created quite a stir, though. It's already excited some international interest.'

'Oh?' Mum sounded dazed and confused.

'So far, the film is all we've got,' Sylvia finished. 'None of the other cameras recorded anything of interest, and we didn't pick up anything on audio, either. But we'll keep looking. Have there been any further developments, Judy?'

'Well – no,' Mum replied. 'Not as such.'

'Yes, there have,' I interrupted. 'The story's started again.'

'I beg your pardon?' said Sylvia. 'Is that you, Judy?'

'It's Alethea,' Mum growled. 'Alethea, get off the phone. You know what I've told you about eaves-dropping.'

'But I have to tell her, Mum. It's probably important.'

'Tell me what?' asked Sylvia, and I explained. For the past few days, I had been finding it more and more difficult to read the writing on the bedroom walls. Once again, white space was running out, and lines were being written over. But I had pieced together just enough to know that Princess Emilie had arrived at the sea-cliff just as Count Osric was sailing towards it. The wind howled. The waves heaved. The ship was making for a headland *hardly ever navigated, where treacherous shoals and breakers were illumined by the refulgent beam of no friendly lighthouse.*

What would happen? Would the ship founder? I was desperate to find out – I'd had a hard time getting to sleep, just thinking about it, perhaps because I was expecting that the end of the story might somehow solve our own problem with Eglantine. But when I checked the walls that morning, I had discovered a very curious thing. There, scribbled on one of the few remaining strips of white wall, were the words, *Once there lived in a bleak clime a white-bearded king.*

'The story is starting again,' I told Sylvia. 'Eglantine's gone back to the beginning, and she didn't even finish it the first time. What do you think that means?'

'I've no idea,' Sylvia replied. 'But perhaps you've simply mixed things up a little, do you think? All those lines of text – they must get very confusing.'

'I haven't mixed up *anything*,' was my stubborn reply. But Sylvia wasn't interested. She told me to keep up the good work, and started talking about the British chapter of the Society for Psychical Research, and how she might consider contacting its president.

So I went away and tackled the question by myself. Why hadn't Eglantine finished the fairy-tale? Why had she started it again? Didn't she *know* what had happened to Count Osric and Princess Emilie? The walls of Bethan's bedroom were turning black once more; looking up at them, I wondered if Eglantine was fated to keep writing the same story over and over again, without ever reaching an end. It was a horrible idea. It made me feel sick in my stomach.

Suddenly I thought: what if I *gave* her an end to the story? Would that make her stop?

As soon as this notion occurred to me, I began to get all hot and excited. I rushed back into my bedroom, grabbed my journal, and hid myself away in Ray's studio. At first I couldn't concentrate. I was too thrilled by my own brilliance.

But after a while I began to calm down, and turned my attention to the text of Eglantine's fairytale.

It had reached the point where Princess Emilie was watching Count Osric's ship lurch and roll towards her through the stormy darkness. *A red light gleamed.* But how was she supposed to get from the cliff to the ship? If Count Osric had ever explained his plan to her, the words had been lost in a dense thicket of scribble.

I had to work it out for myself.

From high above the sea, I wrote, *Emilie could see a boat being launched from the ship.* (Then I realised that it was the middle of a stormy night; how could anyone see anything if it was pitch black?) *There were lanterns on the boat,* I added, *which glittered as it approached her across the waves. Finally the boat reached the cliff. She could see Count Osric. He threw a rope, and she caught it. She tied it to a tree. Then he climbed up the rope, and she threw herself into his arms. "Oh my love!" she cried. "How long I have waited!"* (That was pretty good, don't you think?) *After kissing her, he carried her back to the boat, and sailed away.*

And they lived happily ever after.

It took me about half an hour to write this, and even then I wasn't happy. No matter how much I fiddled with it, I couldn't seem to make it any better. What's more, I had homework to do. So at last I gave up, and copied out my ending, and stuck it to the wall of Bethan's bedroom. I didn't tell anyone about it. I wanted to surprise Mum if anything good *did* happen.

The next morning (Tuesday), I got up early. I was really excited. I went into Bethan's room and looked around, half-expecting the writing on the walls to have vanished during the night.

It hadn't, though. Things were worse – much worse. With dismay, I saw that Eglantine had even scrawled over the piece of paper with my ending on it. She had written, *his domain was almost entirely surrounded by the sea*.

Obviously, she still wasn't satisfied.

Chapter Nine

A lot of things happened on Tuesday.

To begin with, Bethan's photo appeared in the local newspaper. I discovered this at lunchtime, when I spoke to Mrs Procter, the librarian. I had brought a copy of Eglantine's fairytale to school, because it had occurred to me: what if the story was a genuine fairytale? What if it was in a book somewhere? What if Eglantine had been reading the book before she died, and had never finished it?

Clearly, the ending that I'd tacked onto the story hadn't been the right one. But there was a good chance that I might be able to *find* the right ending – with Mrs Procter's help.

So I went to her, and showed her the fairytale,

and asked her if she recognised it.

She looked at it for a moment before remarking, 'Is this something you got off your bedroom wall?'

I stared at her in astonishment. How had she heard about our bedroom wall? Seeing my expression, she hurried to explain.

'It was in the paper, this morning,' she said. 'Didn't you see it? Look – I was reading it on the bus.' She poked around behind her desk and produced a copy of the *News*. On the fourth page was a picture of Bethan in his bedroom, under the words *Local haunting investigated*.

'Oh – I'm sorry, it's your *brother's* bedroom,' she added, peering at the caption under Bethan's black-and-white feet. Behind him, the writing on the walls was faint and blurry.

The story mentioned PRISM, and the possibility that a chemical reaction was responsible for our 'mysterious trouble'. Mum was quoted, but nobody else. I wasn't even named.

'It must be very difficult for you,' said Mrs Procter, studying me closely, and I flushed. I didn't want her to think that we were a family of weirdos.

'Well, it is strange,' I mumbled. 'But there's probably a logical explanation.'

'Yes, of course.'

'The writing was there before we moved in. It just

came back after the room was painted, that's all.'

'But it is some kind of text? Some kind of story? That's the impression I got.'

In reply, I pointed to my copy of the fairytale, which filled twenty-two pages of an exercise book.

'That's as much as I've been able to collect,' I said. 'But it isn't finished. I wanted to know if you'd seen it anywhere else. In a book of some kind.'

'I see.' Mrs Procter flicked through the pages, frowning. 'Of course I'll read it, Alethea. Maybe it will ring a bell.'

'I think it's a fairytale. Mum thinks it's Victorian.'

'I see.'

'It would be good if we could – well – work out the ending.'

I didn't want to tell her why. In fact I left the library, then, and went to join Michelle under the staffroom windows. It's the only safe part of the playground at lunchtime, because of all the rowdy boys and flying tennis balls that make the rest of the playground such a miserable place. I felt too embarrassed to hang around Mrs Procter. I knew what she must have been thinking. And I also knew that things could only get worse, because most people read the local paper on Tuesday afternoon, not Tuesday morning. Just about every teacher at school would have read or heard about Eglantine by the time Wednesday rolled around.

My own teacher, Mr Lee, might start to wonder if I was as sensible as he'd always thought.

When I got home, I saw the local paper on the kitchen table (opened at Bethan's picture) and almost cried. Bethan, of course, was thrilled. Mum also seemed strangely pleased. But before I could point out that the stupid story had practically *ruined* my *life*, Mum drew my attention to a large, yellow envelope that was sitting near the newspaper, under her car keys.

'It's from the Registry of Births, Deaths and Marriages,' she said. 'I think your certificate must have come.'

She was right. When I tore open the envelope, I found inside it a copy of Eglantine May Higgins's death certificate. It told me that she had been seventeen years old at the time of her death; that she had been born in Glebe, New South Wales; that she had been buried at Rookwood Cemetery on the fifth of June, 1907; that her mother (whose maiden name had been Henrietta Botts) had belonged to the Church of England, and that her father had worked for the Bank of New South Wales.

It also told me that Eglantine Higgins had died from 'heart failure, deriving from a severe case of anorexia hysterica'.

'What's anorexia hysterica?' I asked Mum, after glancing over the certificate. She looked up from

Bethan's photograph, and frowned.

'Beg your pardon?' she said.

'Eglantine died of heart failure deriving from a severe case of anorexia hysterica. Do you know what that means?'

'Let me see.' Mum took the certificate. She studied it carefully. Then she said, 'I'm not sure. I suppose anorexia hysterica is something like anorexia nervosa.'

'What's anorexia nervosa?'

'Well, it's . . . well, *you* know, Allie. It's that thing that teenage girls get, where they starve themselves.'

'Oh, *that*.' Of course I knew about that. Tilly Smith's sister had it. 'But I thought it was a new thing, because of all the skinny models in advertising. Did they really have it back in 1907?'

'I don't know. Maybe anorexia hysterica was different. Maybe you should check the dictionary.'

So I did. And I didn't find anorexia hysterica. Under 'anorexy' I found 'want of appetite'. Under 'anorexia nervosa' I found 'a condition in which loss of appetite due to severe emotional disturbance results in emaciation'. Under 'emaciated' I found 'lean or wasted in flesh'. Skinny, in other words. *Very* skinny.

But what about anorexia hysterica?

'Maybe it's another term for anorexia nervosa,'

Ray said that night at the dinner table. 'It sounds like it might be.'

'I'll look up the dictionary at school tomorrow,' I remarked. 'That dictionary's a *big* dictionary. Not like ours.'

'So Eglantine wasn't strangled after all?' Bethan inquired, sounding almost disappointed.

'No, sweetie.' Mum reached for the salt. 'She died of heart failure, poor thing – probably because she was starving herself.'

'Why was she starving herself?' asked Bethan, and Mum replied that she didn't know. Some girls did that, for some reason. It was a strange kind of sickness. But she hadn't realised that girls used to do it in Edwardian times.

'Of course, anorexia hysterica might be a slightly different thing from anorexia nervosa,' Mum went on. Suddenly her eyes widened. 'You know,' she said, turning to Ray, 'I remember reading about the suffragettes. When they went on their hunger strikes, they were force-fed. With a tube.'

'What are suffragettes?' I wanted to know.

'What's force-fed?' asked Bethan.

'So what's your point?' said Ray, and Mum exclaimed, 'The *dream*, Ray! Bethan's dream!'

'Oh.'

'Maybe the poor girl had a tube stuck down her

throat. So they could pour milk down it, or some-thing.'

'What's a suffragette?' I repeated doggedly. Mum explained that suffragettes were women who had fought for 'universal suffrage' – that is, for a woman's right to vote in political elections. In England, many women had been gaoled for doing things like chaining themselves to fences and shouting in parliament. In prison, they had often refused to eat – in protest – and had been force-fed as a result.

'Yuk,' I said. 'That's terrible.'

'Yes.'

'Did it happen in Australia, too?'

'I don't know.' Mum thought for a minute. 'I don't think so. I think women already had the vote in Australia, by then.'

That pleased me. And the next day I felt even more pleased when I went to the school library, at lunchtime, and found a book on anorexia nervosa. Finding that book gave me a real sense of achieve-ment – until I opened it up.

Then I discovered that girls who get anorexia are often moody, sensitive to the needs of others, desperate for approval, highly intelligent, and angry with their brothers and sisters. That made me nervous. It was not only a possible description of Eglantine – it was also a possible description of me! I thought to myself, no *way* am I ever going to become a vegetarian. I need my *meat*. I don't want to get anorexia. From now on, I'm going to *demand* a chocolate bar every day, and I'm never going to *look* at another issue of *Teen*. (Not that I'd be caught dead reading *Teen*, but you know what I'm saying.) I also resolved to be nicer to Bethan. Oh, and to stop caring what Mr Lee thought about me. So what if he had read the local newspaper? So what if he knew that I believed in ghosts? As long as he kept giving me good marks, his opinion of me wouldn't *really* make any difference. (Would it?)

Of course, I'm not in the least bit *desperate* for approval. I don't care what any of the dumb kids at school think of me. I won't let Michelle paint my fingernails, no matter how much she begs. But still . . . it made me think. It really made me think.

I was thinking, in fact, when I happened to glance at the index of the book I was reading, and saw the words 'anorexia hysterica'. Naturally, I went straight to the pages listed, and found out that anorexia hysterica was a term used by Victorian doctors to describe anorexia nervosa. I also found out that the condition had first been identified in 1868. Typical sufferers, I read, were from the higher walks of society, well-educated, and prone to a 'morbid perversion of the will'. They often read too much. (Doctors at the time thought that young women shouldn't read too much, because it damaged their health, made them overly romantic and destroyed their appetites.) Girls of a 'nervous character' were told not to consume tea, coffee, chocolate, spices and nuts, in case such things made them worse.

Girls like this often wanted to be spiritual, and delicate. They wanted to be like the poet Lord Byron, who had lived on biscuits and soda water for days at a time. Sometimes they stopped eating after they'd had a 'romantic disappointment'. Sometimes they stopped eating because everything else they did was watched, controlled and commented upon.

The chapter called 'Fasting Girls' mentioned Mollie Fancher, who lived in America in the 1870s, and ate almost nothing at all. 'Her books were her delight,' a friend of Mollie's said. 'She neglected all for them.' I read that Mollie had been force-fed with a stomach pump. Lots of girls with anorexia were fed with stomach pumps, sometimes at home, sometimes after being sent to a mental asylum. They were also given electric shocks.

I thought about Eglantine, as I read all this. I thought about how she must have had a tube forced down her throat, and milk pumped into her stomach. According to the book, people with anorexia finally reach the stage where they *can't* absorb food, because their stomachs don't work any more. At this stage they're always thirsty, always constipated, and always cold. Their skin is pale and dry. They get dizzy when they stand, and have to lie down a lot. They become hairy all over.

I imagined what it must have been like for Eglantine. I imagined her lying in Bethan's bedroom, wrapped in layers and layers of heavy clothing, being offered milk, cream, soup, eggs, fish or chicken every two hours. (This, according to the book, was the recommended diet for girls with anorexia.) I imagined her hairy arms and her pale, thin face. Had she suffered from a 'romantic disappointment'? Had she been nursing a broken heart?

I thought about Princess Emilie and Count Osric. I thought about the words written on the flyleaf of *Idylls of the King*: *A good book is the precious lifeblood of a master spirit, embalmed and treasured up on purpose to a life beyond life.* Eglantine had liked books, just as Mollie Fancher had. Perhaps she had liked them too much. Perhaps she had 'neglected all for them'.

I could picture Eglantine lying in her bed, cold and thirsty, with nothing to do but read. Her thin, pale fingers would have leafed through *Idylls of the King*, and through the story of Princess Emilie. Perhaps that story had dropped from her hands unfinished because she was too weak to read any more. I felt quite upset when I considered that possibility. I had to blow my nose very hard. Poor Eglantine. Poor, poor Eglantine. Had she really starved herself to death because some boy had disappointed her? It seemed so tragic.

'Oh, dear,' said Mum, when I told her of my discoveries that afternoon. 'How awful. No wonder the *chi* in that room is so bad.'

'They probably gave her electric shocks. Why would they do that, do you think?'

'I don't know. But, Allie, you mustn't fret over things like this. I really don't want you *dwelling* on it. It's morbid.'

'Morbid?'

'Unwholesome. Sickly.'

'The Victorian doctors called anorexia a "morbid perversion of the will".'

'Well, and so it is, don't you think? You have to have a lot of willpower to starve yourself to death.' Mum frowned, suddenly, and cocked her head. 'I suppose it's not surprising that Eglantine died of anorexia,' she went on, thoughtfully. 'Because when you think about it, only a person with a lot of willpower would have the strength of spirit to keep on going after she died.' With a sigh, Mum blinked, and glanced over at the draining board. '*I* don't even have enough willpower to wash the dishes in the morning,' she added.

'Do you think it would help if we left some water in the bedroom overnight?' I asked. 'Do you think the ghost is just thirsty? Or hungry, maybe?'

'I don't know, Al.' Another sigh. 'Perhaps we'd better ask the Feng Shui master. He's coming on Thursday night.'

Chapter Ten

The Feng Shui man was not Chinese. He was called Bryce McGarrigle. But he was quite solemn and quite old (at least, I *think* he was old: he was going bald, and his face was full of creases), and he was wearing a shirt with Chinese writing embroidered on the breast pocket. So I suppose that he was the next best thing to Chinese.

He came after dinner, while we were eating Ray's macaroons. He didn't say much. When Mum offered him some macaroons and jasmine tea, he thanked her; he also complimented her on the kitchen's *bagua*. Mostly, however, he just listened. He listened while Mum described our problems, sipping his tea, nodding sometimes, his pouchy grey eyes fixed on a point in the centre of the kitchen table.

When Mum had finished, he said, 'You tried offering food and drink?'

'Last night,' Mum replied. 'But it didn't seem to work.'

'And you tried a purification ritual?'

'Yes.'

'Of what nature?'

Mum told him. He nodded again. Then he got up and went to look at Bethan's bedroom.

Naturally, we all followed him. But he was so thorough that we became impatient. After studying the rooms upstairs, he circled the outside of the house, examined the plumbing, and generally spent so much time counting steps, peering over fences and measuring windows that Bethan and I finally wandered away. Bethan plonked himself down in front of the TV, while I tackled my homework.

It was at least an hour before I heard Mum and Mr McGarrigle talking, next door, in Bethan's bedroom.

'. . . this room is in the thunder *bagua* of the second floor,' Mr McGarrigle was saying, 'but it's also swallowing a lot of your Tai Chi unity. And that's being aggravated by the position of the house itself.'

'Oh, dear,' said Mum. 'How?'

101

Mr McGarrigle explained that the house next door, being taller than ours and built on rising ground, was inflicting a fair degree of 'downward energy' on us. We could cure that, of course, with a concave mirror – and the cutting *chi* of the intersection opposite our house could also be reversed by the placement of a mirror, or a very shiny brass knob, on the front door.

'But your real problem lies in this room,' Mr McGarrigle continued. 'There is far too much thunder energy in this room. To begin with, it's facing east, which doesn't help, though you can't do much about that. You *can* oil the door hinges. You *can* get rid of that drum. What is it? Javanese?'

'It was a present from Bethan's father,' said Mum, in a dazed voice.

'Then put it somewhere else. No musical instruments in this room. And I suggest you fill in that fireplace – I don't suppose you use it, do you?'

'Well, no . . .'

'Then fill it in. The last thing you need in this room is extra space in the thunder area of its *bagua*. The thunder energy in here is so aggressive, it's swallowing your Tai Chi unity. And unity includes the balance between the world of the flesh and the world of the spirit.'

Mr McGarrigle went on like this for quite a long time. He talked about elders, and mirrors, and negative spaces. He talked about the Three-Door Gate of Chi and the theory of the Five Trans-formations. Then he announced that he intended to carry out his own purification ritual, which might take several hours. He had brought the right equipment – it was in the car – but he would be grateful if Mum could drape all the sharp corners in Bethan's room with soft fabrics.

'You – you mean you're going to do it now?' Mum stammered.

'The sooner the better. The energy in this room is *very* unstable.'

Poor Mum. It was a weekday night, and she wanted to get to bed early. She wanted *everyone* in bed early. But Mr McGarrigle kept trudging up and down the stairs, fetching noisy things from his car and water from the kitchen, and then he began to burn something, in Bethan's bedroom, that smelled pretty strange. I can't describe it, exactly, but it was certainly pungent. Soon the whole upstairs landing stank of it, even though Bethan's bedroom door was shut.

Bethan refused to go to bed, as a result. 'I can't breathe up there,' he grumbled.

'Oh, Bethan, it's not that bad,' said Mum.

'Yes, it is.'

'Do you think a bad smell is going to drive Eglantine away?' I asked doubtfully.

'It's not a bad smell, Allie, it's a *purifying* smell,' said Mum, and Bethan rolled his eyes.

'Just close your door and leave your window open,' Ray advised me. But Bethan pointed out it wasn't just the smell – it was the noise. Mr McGarrigle was chanting something in a low, rumbling voice that sounded like a plane engine. How could anyone get to sleep with a plane revving its engine in the next room?

'You just want to stay up late, so you can watch *Star Trek: Voyager*,' Mum said in a steely voice. 'Don't think you're going to do *that*, Bethan.'

And he didn't. We were both in bed by ten o'clock, despite all Bethan's efforts. The chanting had stopped by then, and the smell was different – a flowery, citrussy kind of smell that wasn't too bad. Bethan dropped off immediately (as he always does). I was just beginning to fall asleep when all at once there was a terrific shriek from the next room.

A shriek, a clang and a thump that made the floor shake.

I was out of bed before I knew what I was doing. Out of bed, out the door and onto the landing.

Mr McGarrigle was there, draped over the banisters.

'What is it?' I cried. 'What happened?'

He was gasping and groaning. As Mum and Ray

pounded up the stairs, Bethan called out from the bedroom.

'What's going on?' he demanded thickly.

'Oh – oh . . .' said Mr McGarrigle.

'Bryce? What's wrong?' Mum demanded. But Mr McGarrigle couldn't talk. He kept coughing and clearing his throat.

I stepped into Bethan's bedroom. A kind of lamp was burning on the floor. A silver bowl had been knocked over, and water spilled. There were little heaps of things: smooth pebbles, flower petals, salt, rice.

'I – I was meditating,' Mr McGarrigle said hoarsely. 'In a trance. I – when I reached the second plane, I –'

'What?' said Mum, as Mr McGarrigle paused.

'Someone tried to choke me!' he cried. His voice sounded quite different: high and wobbly, when it had once been low and calm. 'I couldn't – I couldn't breathe!'

'Oh, dear,' said Mum. Ray and I exchanged nervous glances.

Eglantine's stomach pump, obviously.

'God,' Mr McGarrigle panted. 'God, it was appalling.'

'Come downstairs,' Mum pleaded, timidly patting his shoulder. 'Come and have a cup of tea.'

'God. I've never – this has never happened before.'

'I'm so sorry . . .'

They stumbled downstairs together, arm in arm. Ray followed them.

Once again, I looked around Bethan's bedroom. It was dark and gloomy; the light was turned off, and the walls were almost completely black. The single flame dancing on the wick of Mr McGarrigle's lamp made shadows leap and flicker.

Everything was shrouded in sheets and towels.

'Eglantine!' I said, in a loud, angry, trembling voice. 'Eglantine, you horrible person, go away! We don't want you here! You're a *nasty piece of work!*'

'Who are you talking to?' Bethan mumbled from behind me. He'd got up at last, and was standing, bleary-eyed, with his hair on end, holding up his pyjama pants.

'Eglantine,' I replied. 'I was talking to Eglantine.'

'Why? What's happened?'

'Oh . . . nothing. Nothing much.' I tried to tell myself that it had only been another stomach-pump dream, after all. Just a dream. Nothing to be afraid of.

Though it did occur to me that the stomach-pump dream might feel a lot more real if you weren't asleep when you dreamed it.

'Go back to bed, okay?' I said hoarsely. 'The Feng Shui man is finished.'

I was right, too. Mr McGarrigle didn't come back. Ray told me later that he had washed his hands of the whole business. He had left the house a changed man – not solemn and silent but nervy and babbling and shrill. He had, however, promised to find Mum a good psychic. That's what she needed, he said – either that or she should move house.

'I really think we're going to have to,' Mum moaned later. 'We can't go on like this, how can we? We can't live here while Eglantine's in charge.'

'She won't be for much longer,' Ray said. 'We'll get rid of her, I know we will.'

'But *how*, Ray? How?'

He didn't have an answer. I didn't have an answer. I wished that I did, because it made me feel weird to see Mum so upset. In fact, I now felt more angry with Eglantine than sorry for her.

Fortunately, Mr McGarrigle called Mum the next day with the name of a psychic, and a question about finger-cymbals. Had he left his finger-cymbals in Bethan's bedroom? No? Oh, dear. Then he must have dropped them somewhere on the way to his car.

We had some other calls on Friday, too.

The first was from Richard Boyer. He rang up to

report that, so far, the chemical engineer consulted about Eglantine's writing hadn't made much progress. He had a few ideas, but couldn't prove any of them without something concrete to work with. Would it be all right if Richard came back and removed a small piece of Bethan's bedroom wall? Or perhaps just took some paint samples?

Mum replied that she would think about it and get back to him.

The second call was from a member of the Australian Ghost Hunters Society, who said that he had read about our case on the 'Strange Nation' website, a site which monitored Australian media for stories about hauntings, UFO spottings, and anything else that might defy logical explanation. Our case, he explained, had been mentioned – briefly – because someone must have read our local newspaper. When asked how he had tracked down our telephone number, he replied that it hadn't been hard, because he had our name and suburb. Now, could he ask Mum, please, exactly what the *content* of our 'automatic writings' might be?

Mum referred him to Richard Boyer.

The third and last call was from a television journalist. Her name was Bryony Birtles, and she was doing research for Channel Nine. She had heard about our case, and had already talked to Sylvia Klineberg. Would it be okay if she were to talk to Mum? Maybe she could come around, and have a look at Bethan's bedroom walls? Just as a sort of research trip, to see if the story was worth pursuing.

Mum, to my surprise, was rather cautious. She said she didn't know. She said she would have to talk to the family. She promised that she would call back with an answer.

Then she confessed to me that she was beginning to wonder if things were getting out of hand. She didn't like the idea of people reading about us on the internet, and calling us out of the blue. It was unnerving.

'I don't know what to do,' she said. 'I really don't know what to do.'

I didn't, either. So far, Mrs Procter hadn't been any help. She told me at lunchtime that she hadn't been able to find Eglantine's fairytale anywhere. But she promised to fax it through to her old English lecturer, who was an 'expert' on Victorian literature. If the fairytale existed anywhere, he would be able to find it, she said.

Meanwhile, I would just have to sit and wait.

'One thing I *do* think we should do,' said Mum, 'is paint Bethan's room again. I really think we should do that tomorrow.'

Ray paused in the act of winding spaghetti around his fork. 'Why?' he asked. 'What's the point? I'm sure it won't do any good. The writing will just come back again.'

'Yes, but it's *black* now, Ray. The room is black – have you looked at it, lately? And black is a bad colour. It's associated with inactivity: stagnant water energy. Death. Diminishment. In the psyche, black plays the role of the shadow figure. Whereas white is the colour of healing and purifying.'

Ray sighed. 'So you want *me* to paint it again. Is that right?' he said.

'Please.'

He couldn't say no, though he wasn't happy. He went to bed grumpy, and Mum went to bed worried. Bethan went to bed and snored. Talk about thunder energy. Even when I threw a pillow at his head, he didn't wake up.

I felt like stuffing something up his nose – or down his throat. And I wondered gloomily if that was Eglantine's problem. Perhaps she just didn't like it when people snored.

I dreamed about Eglantine, that night, though it wasn't the stomach-pump dream. I dreamed of a hand – Eglantine's hand. It was pale and thin. There was too much hair on it. All I could see was the hand, with a frill of lace around its wrist, holding a pen. It was writing and writing. It went on and on. But it wasn't writing on a wall.

It was writing in a journal, like mine. A bound book of blank pages – blank, white pages. The writing was familiar. The words were familiar.

I woke to the sound of Mum screaming, and fell over as I rushed, half-asleep, to the door.

It was morning. The sun was up. Mum stood on the landing, shaking from head to foot. When I grabbed her arm, and begged to know what was wrong, she pointed.

Eglantine had written a new line of text. But it wasn't inside Bethan's room.

It was on the wall of the landing.

Chapter Eleven

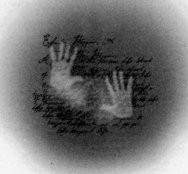

'**We've got to** leave!' Mum gabbled. 'We've got to leave this house *now!*'

'No, we don't,' said Ray. 'Calm down, Judy.'

'Didn't you see? Ray, it's *escaped out of the room!*'

'And do you know why? Because the walls of that room are black, now.' Ray stirred sugar into Mum's coffee and brought it over to her. She was sitting at the kitchen table. 'You can't see what's written inside that room any more,' he said, 'so the writing's moved outside it. All we have to do is paint the room again. Like you said. Then it will move back inside.'

'But it *can* get out, Ray! This means that it *can* get out! It might be roaming all over the house every night. It might have been in our *bedroom!*'

Bethan began to snivel. I was so surprised that I put my arm around him.

'Look,' said Ray. He spoke quite sternly. Even though he's not very big, and wears glasses, and hasn't got much in the way of muscles, he looked quite scary, then. He looked like someone that no one – not even Eglantine – should be messing with.

'Look,' he said, 'let's not overreact, eh? Let's not start frightening each other. Judy? This isn't useful.'

Mum blinked. She glanced at Bethan, and cleared her throat, and said, 'No. Okay. Um . . . right.'

'First of all, we should have breakfast and get dressed,' Ray went on. 'Then I'll go and get some white paint, and you can ring Trish or the psychic or whoever you want to ring, and we'll decide what to do from there. Okay?'

'Okay,' said Mum. 'It was that wretched Bryce. He got me all worked up.'

'I know,' Ray replied, soothingly. 'It's all right, kids. We'll sort it out. Now . . .' He took a deep breath. 'Anyone for pancakes?'

After breakfast, I went back upstairs. My hands were shaking as I studied the line on the landing wall (*So the smooth-faced boy that came the morrow eve*)

113

before entering Bethan's bedroom again. Stepping into it was like stepping into a cave. The walls and ceiling were black, with pinpricks of white paint showing through here and there, like stars in a night sky. All the little piles of pebbles and rice and stuff had been taken away. So had the sheets that had been draped over Bethan's furniture.

'What do you want?' I said aloud, trying to stop my voice from shaking the way my hands were. I was on the verge of tears. For the first time, I was feeling . . . not frightened, exactly, but anxious. Very, very anxious. 'Eglantine? What *is* it, with you?'

And then I remembered my dream.

I remembered the hand, writing, writing, writing. In a journal, not on a wall. In a *book*.

Perhaps Eglantine hadn't been *reading* the fairy-tale after all. Perhaps she had been writing it because it was her *own* story, out of her own head, but she hadn't been able to finish it before she died.

Perhaps she was *obsessed* with the story, and couldn't rest in peace until she'd finished it.

I leaned against the wall, thinking hard. It seemed to make sense. I wasn't a writer myself, but I was a reader and a solver of puzzles. I knew how hard it was, sometimes, to let something go. To put a book down, turn off the light, and fall asleep.

I remembered all the times I'd taken a torch to bed, so that I could secretly finish something. I remembered how often I'd lain awake, turning words or numbers or plots around and around in my head. What if Eglantine had been the same? What if she had felt the same about writing stories as I sometimes did about reading them? What if she had felt absolutely *compelled* to get the words out of her mind, onto the page?

I remembered what Mum had said about Eglantine's willpower. Perhaps the full force of her will had been directed towards finishing and publishing her story, so that she would become famous. Or maybe in the hope that the boy who had disappointed her would read her story, and feel ashamed that he hadn't loved her as much as Osric had loved Emilie.

Maybe I was right. Maybe I'd found the root of the problem. But even if I had, what good would it do me? Because, after all, I couldn't finish the story for her. I'd tried already, and it hadn't worked. If an ending was what she wanted, I couldn't supply the right kind of ending. I didn't see how *anybody* could. Not if the story had been coming out of her own head.

I went downstairs and looked very carefully through *Idylls of the King*, but it was no good. Eglantine hadn't marked it with a single note or comment of any kind – except her name, and the date, and the quote from Milton.

'Don't run away with that,' Mum remarked, as she passed me on her way out the door. 'The psychic's coming tonight, and she said it would help if we had any personal items. Belonging to Eglantine.'

'Oh!' I said. 'You mean you've rung the psychic?'

'I've rung the psychic. I told her it was an emergency.'

'Do you think she can help?'

'She said she'd try. She said she's had one or two successes in the past.' Mum paused, with her hand on the doorknob. 'I'm going shopping. Is there anything you need, specially?'

My own bedroom, I thought, but didn't say it aloud.

'I'd prefer it if you didn't touch that book,' she added, pulling open the front door. 'God knows where it's been, Allie. Ray's right – we should have burned it.'

'But then what would the psychic have used?'

'I don't know. I don't care.'

'Mum! Wait!' She was halfway down the front path, so I stuck my head out the window. 'Mum, what's the psychic's name?'

'Delora Starburn.'

Delora Starburn! I wondered if it was a made-up

name, and decided that it probably was. I wondered what sort of person gave herself a name like that, and pictured someone very much like Trish, only with wilder hair.

I was wrong, though. Delora Starburn didn't look a bit like Trish. When she arrived, late that afternoon, she was wearing pink leather trousers (with legs on them that ended halfway down her calves), very high heels, a jacket trimmed with fake fur, and *lots* of makeup. Her hair was long and blond, except where a streak of darker hair showed at the parting. Her skin was so tanned that it had almost cracked in places; she had a square face and a rough, squawking voice like a cockatoo's. Her breath smelled of cigarette smoke.

'Hello, sweetie,' she beamed when I opened the front door. 'Is your mum home? She's expecting me.'

'Are you the –?'

'I'm Delora. Who are you?'

My first thought was: shouldn't you already know who I am? Being a psychic, and everything? But of course I didn't say it.

'I'm Alethea.'

'What a gorgeous name! Oh, hello. Judy, is it? I'm Delora.'

For the next ten minutes, Delora talked nonstop. She clattered down the hall, exclaiming

117

over 'this gorgeous, gorgeous house'. When she was introduced to Richard Boyer, who had wanted to be on hand during our 'psychical experiment', she practically shrieked with delight, declared that he must be a Virgo ('Am I right? I knew it!'), and launched into a long, confusing story about her cousin's computer, which had 'gremlins' in it that were destroying her cousin's life work. She even managed to talk while she was drinking a glass of wine. Clacking about on her high heels, she cooed over Mum's Tasmanian-ash kitchen cup-boards and explained that she was late because there had been a pile-up on the freeway, and a huge traffic jam.

'Oh, *thank* you, sweetie!' she exclaimed, when I presented her with *Idylls of the King*. 'This was hers, you say? Oh, good.'

'There's her name,' I pointed out, turning to the flyleaf.

'Yes, I see. I didn't even know if I'd make it at *all*, because my car, I tell you, it's falling apart, it's such a *bomb* . . .'

Everyone sat around dumbly as she raved on. We were trying to be polite, but wondering all the time when she was actually going to knuckle down and do some work. Finally, however, she finished her wine, set the glass down on the kitchen table, and declared, 'Right. I'll be back in a minute.'

Then she left the room. We could hear her noisy heels on the staircase.

'What's she doing?' Bethan asked Mum.

'I – I don't know.' Mum looked at Ray. 'Do you think – I mean –'

'She's probably going to the toilet,' Ray retorted, drily. 'Don't worry. She'll be back. There's no one up there to talk to.'

'She's not at all what I expected,' Mum remarked, and turned to Richard. 'Are psychics usually like that?'

But Richard just giggled nervously, and shrugged, and pushed his glasses up his nose.

'Well . . . I suppose I'd better get on with dinner,' Mum sighed. 'Thank God it's spaghetti. Looks as if we might be feeding *her*, as well.'

Delora was upstairs for nearly an hour. After about fifteen minutes, Mum began to get worried, but Ray told her not to fret, because if Delora needed anything, she would certainly ask for it. ('I don't think she'd be backward in coming forward,' he said.) At six o'clock, Mum served up the spaghetti and salad, insisting that Richard join us, even though he protested that he didn't want to put her to any trouble. As we ate, we kept listening for footsteps on the stairs. Mum, I think, listened particularly hard; at one point she made a comment about Delora stealing her jewellery, and she was only half-joking.

Nobody else talked much. Richard told us a story about an English goldsmith named Frederick Thompson, who in 1905 suddenly found himself painting pictures. At the same time, he began to suffer from hallucinations – visions of country scenes – which became the subjects of these pictures. A year after he started to paint, he went to an exhibition of works by an artist named Robert Swain Gifford, who had died some years earlier. He heard a voice in his head say, 'You see what I have done. Can you not take up and finish my work?'

It was soon discovered that Frederick's paintings closely resembled scenes which had been well known to the painter Robert Gifford – but which Frederick himself had never seen.

'Lordy,' said Ray, when Richard had finished. 'I hope *I* don't start getting hallucinations. That's all I need.'

'The moment *anyone* starts getting hallucinations, we're moving house,' Mum declared. Then she caught her breath, as high heels sounded overhead. They began to rap briskly down the stairs, signalling Delora's return.

We waited anxiously, our mouths full of food.

'Well,' Delora said brightly, upon entering the kitchen. 'That was interesting.' I noticed that, despite her encouraging smile, she looked different. Less bouncy. Her eyes seemed tired – almost dazed – and her hair was ruffled. Her wrinkles were more obvious.

'There's a *massive* amount of disruption up there, really massive,' she went on, collapsing into a chair. Gratefully, she accepted Mum's offer of another glass of wine. 'I could feel it the minute I walked in.'

'That room has an electromagnetic reading of point twelve,' Richard observed, but Delora didn't seem to hear. She swallowed a mouthful of wine, shut her eyes, massaged her forehead, and continued.

'Did you say that this girl – this Eglantine – did you say that she died of starvation?'

'Yes,' I replied, when no one else did.

'Well, that's odd.' Delora was frowning. Her eyes were still shut. 'Because I would almost have thought that she'd drowned. I had the impression of someone falling into water.'

'Water?' said Mum. 'You mean, like bathwater?'

'No. Like the sea.' Delora opened her eyes. 'A heavy sea, near a cliff. Did Eglantine ever fall into the sea?'

I sat up straight. I swallowed. Can you guess what I was thinking?

'No,' I croaked, 'but I bet Emilie did.'

Everyone turned to look at me.

'Emilie is the character in Eglantine's fairytale,'

I explained, and gave everyone a quick sketch of the unfinished story. 'It ended up with Emilie waiting for Osric on the edge of a cliff,' I said, 'while he battled with a storm. If Emilie fell into the sea, it would be an unhappy ending. No wonder Eglantine didn't like the ending that I wrote – she wanted something like Romeo and Juliet.' I then revealed my theory about Eglantine being a writer, unable to rest until her story was complete. 'Maybe the only way to get rid of her,' I concluded, 'is to help her write the end of the story.'

For a while, nobody spoke. Bethan kept stuffing food into his mouth, but he did it slowly, without taking his eyes off my face. Ray uttered a drawn-out, long-suffering sigh. Mum chewed on her fingernails. Richard pushed his glasses up his nose and glanced at Delora.

Delora began to nod, thoughtfully.

'Well, that makes sense,' she said. 'Okay. Right. Not a problem.' She stood up. 'Anybody got a pen and paper?'

Startled glances were exchanged.

'What are you going to do?' asked Mum.

'I'm going to help her finish her story. It might take a while, though. Could I have a coffee, do you think, and – oh, something to write on? You got a card table, love, and a little chair?'

Mum stood up slowly, wearing a dazed

expression. So did Ray. They stumbled about, looking for coffee and card tables, while Richard began to gabble on – in his breathy, excited way – about channelling and automatists.

While the card table was being erected in Bethan's bedroom, Richard told me about someone called Mrs Curran, who had produced several astoundingly accurate historical novels between 1910 and 1930, set in periods about which she knew nothing. It was claimed she was simply the tool of a dead woman named Patience Worth, whose words were being 'channelled' through her.

'I guess the same theory applies here,' said Richard, hovering on the stairs. 'I'd like to record it. Do you think Delora would mind being filmed?'

'Ask her,' I rejoined.

So he did. And Delora replied that she'd be *delighted*, nothing would please her more than being stuck all night in a bedroom with Richard Boyer. She fluttered her eyelashes when she said this, and Richard looked a bit startled. I was surprised, too. But after studying him, I decided that he was quite handsome, behind his glasses – he had nice curly hair, at least, and big eyes, and a straight nose. He was younger than Delora, too.

'I won't even *try* to open myself up until the whole house is settled,' Delora told Mum. 'From what you've told me, she only manifests herself when you're all asleep, so she obviously doesn't like a lot of noise and movement. I'll wait until you're in bed, and see what I can do.' She coughed into her nicotine-stained fingers. 'I'm not promising anything, mind you, but I'll do my best.'

'And how much more will this cost?' Mum asked. 'I mean, if you're here the whole night –'

'Oh! Don't worry about that,' Richard interjected. 'I'll pay the extra fee.'

'But Richard –'

'No, no. Really. I want to see this.'

Delora made a noise like someone presented with a particularly yummy piece of chocolate cake, and patted Richard's cheek. 'Gorgeous,' she said. 'I love him. I want to take him home in my purse.' Then she sat down to polish off a bowl of spaghetti, and I went away to do my homework.

For the rest of that evening, until I went to bed, I could hear Delora chattering away downstairs in the kitchen. She was still down there when I drifted off to sleep.

I have to admit that I just couldn't picture Eglantine Higgins getting on with Delora Starburn. By this time, I had a very strong impression of Eglantine Higgins – I thought that she must have been quite serious, and fierce, and clever and poetic – and Delora didn't seem to be any of those things. What's more, Delora never stopped talking. How was she going to hear Eglantine if she never stopped talking?

I was expecting to be awakened as soon as Delora came upstairs. I didn't see how she could sit in the next room with Richard Boyer and not start talking in her cockatoo voice about motorway tolls, or her ex-husband, or renovating old houses. So I was *very* surprised when I woke up the next morning at about half past five and realised I had slept all night through.

Outside, the light was pearly and dim. Bethan was snoring. Quietly, I got out of bed and slipped onto the landing, which was deserted. The door of Bethan's bedroom stood open, but there was no one inside. An empty cup stood on the card table, and Richard's video camera was turned off.

I looked around at the white walls. Ray had painted over them, the day before, and they didn't appear to have been touched since then. At a glance, I couldn't see any new lines of script. But I didn't linger, because at that moment I heard the faint sound of voices from downstairs.

I don't think I've ever made it from the upstairs landing down to the kitchen so quickly.

'Well?' I gasped, throwing myself through the kitchen door. 'What happened?' Even as I spoke, I realised that *something* must have happened. I could tell, just from the atmosphere in that room.

It wasn't tense or excited, though – don't get me wrong. On the contrary, it was incredibly peaceful. Pale sunlight slanted through the window. Cups of coffee steamed gently on the table. Delora and Richard were sitting opposite Mum and Ray, and they all looked terribly tired, but not distressed. They looked tired in a good way.

Mum reached for me.

'Hello, darling,' she said, putting her arm around my waist.

'What happened? Oh!' I had spotted the exercise book lying open in front of her. 'Is that –?'

'Yes.' Mum smiled. 'It's the story. The *whole* story.'

'You mean, from beginning to end?'

'Yes.'

I dragged the book towards me. The writing wasn't familiar – it must have been Delora's. But the words were certainly familiar. *Once there lived in a bleak clime a white-bearded king.*

Hurriedly, I flicked through the pages until I reached the last one. *Morning came, I read, and still the princess stood on the lofty cliff. She saw spars and pieces of the wreck in the sea below. She climbed, by a winding path, down the cliff-side to the beach. She saw Osric lying dead. She saw the men dead around her – in each eye a reproach, and each clammy mouth seeming to say, It is thou!*

She cast herself into the pounding waves, and was never seen again.

'Oh, dear,' I murmured, as my eyes filled with tears. 'So it *was* like Romeo and Juliet.'

'I was only a conduit,' Delora replied dreamily. 'I allowed her inspiration to break through from the spirit realm. It was blocked there. The last lines couldn't push through, because they hadn't manifested themselves here before.'

'It was like Frederick Thompson,' Richard added. 'Like Mrs Curran. I got it all on film. She was amazing, absolutely amazing. The room was pitch black.' He and Delora beamed at each other.

I read the last paragraph. *But now*, it said, *if I should relate that the lady's disappointed affianced went back to his father's realm, where the two made war upon the white-bearded king — ah, how dreamy, and alien, and far away would it not seem? And this because the tale of the lovers is complete. Loves are immortal, just as lovers are. Tales of these, and of these alone, are ever new — because love never dies.*

The End.

'Is there any more writing on the walls?' I asked.

'Not that I could see,' Richard replied.

'Are you sure? Have you checked?'

'You have a look, Allie,' Ray suggested, in a weary but contented kind of way. 'You've got better eyes than we have.'

So I went back upstairs to Bethan's room. Before I left the kitchen, however, I stopped in front of

127

Delora. She must have been smoking, because I could smell it on her breath.

'Did you actually see Eglantine?' I inquired awkwardly. 'Did you – I mean, did you speak to her?' Suddenly, I realised how much I would have loved to speak to her myself. I so badly wanted to ask her questions, look at her face, find out why her story had been the most important thing in her life.

But Delora shook her head.

'I don't know, love,' she said in her husky voice. 'I don't know if I spoke to her. To tell you the truth, I don't remember a thing.'

'You don't remember any of it?'

'Nope. Never do. It's like I go to sleep, and wake up when it's all over.'

I stared at her, and she smiled back at me. Her eyes were small and brown. They looked older than the rest of her.

And the rest of her, I should tell you, looked pretty old in that clear morning light. Even her lips had lines on them.

'Well,' I said, 'you must be . . . I mean, you're very clever.'

'Thanks, love.'

After that, I went upstairs. I looked and looked. I got up on a chair and looked; I got down on my knees and looked. I scanned every centimetre of the walls in Bethan's room, and after half an hour, I had found only one line of script, written under the window.

It said, *The End*.

Chapter Twelve

It was the end, too. Well – it was and it wasn't.
Eglantine did stop writing, so Bethan was able to
move back into his bedroom (which was painted
with another two coats of white paint, just to be
on the safe side). He was a little reluctant, at first,
in case Eglantine was still there, and Mum had to
spend one night in the room herself to reassure
him. When she reported that she'd had no dreams
about choking, he agreed to try out the room
himself. After a week of that, he moved all his toys
out of my room, and things returned to normal –
in one sense.

But in another sense they didn't, because people
were still interested in Eglantine. Richard Boyer

was one of these people. He was very upset when he learned that we had painted over Eglantine's writing on the ceiling of Bethan's bedroom. And we couldn't give him a piece of the bedroom wall to make him feel better, because the wall was made of lath and plaster – not gyprock – and wouldn't have responded well to being hacked about. So Richard was unable to establish, without doubt, that our mysterious writing had been of a para-normal nature.

Nevertheless, it was a case that received a lot of attention. Channel Nine even ran a short item on Eglantine, using Richard's videotape of Delora, and of the single line of script that he had managed to photograph as it slowly appeared on Bethan's bedroom wall. Delora was interviewed, too. She was wearing false fingernails, painted purple, which must have been about ten centimetres long.

Anyway, you can imagine what happened next. We were *swamped* with mail – most of it from weirdos – asking us to interpret their dreams, or requesting permission to visit our house, or describing other examples of haunted rooms. Mum passed all of these letters on to PRISM. In the end, she didn't even bother to read them. She also had to take down the sign that she had put up over the front door not long after the writing stopped. The sign had said *Eglantine*, because all the other houses on our street were called something (like *St Elmo* or *Bideawee*), and she thought it might be nice to name our house after its absent ghost. (I think she was feeling a bit guilty about Eglantine, now that we were rid of her.) But poor Mum hadn't counted on all the stickybeaks. We had people knocking on the front door, asking if ours was 'the haunted house'. We had people hanging around taking pictures, and other people peering through our living-room window. Now, most of the stickybeaks aren't quite sure which terrace is ours.

You must be wondering why Eglantine was suddenly so popular. The fact is, she's now a famous case, like the Borley Rectory hoax. Two months after she disappeared, there were already three hundred and forty-eight references to Eglantine Higgins on the internet, and soon after that we had a call from the producers of an American TV show called 'Stranger than Fiction'. We never saw the program that they made about Eglantine, but they did film us all sitting around the living room and talking about our experiences. (Mum and I did most of the talking; Ray and Bethan just sat.) Because the American show used an Australian camera crew, and Richard Boyer's videotape, and parts of the Channel Nine program, its episode about Eglantine didn't cost very much to make. If it had, I don't suppose the producers would have bothered to make it. But it was interesting for us, and we got paid for taking part – though I don't know how much they paid us, because Mum wouldn't tell me. She did, however, take us out for dinner and a movie to celebrate. So we can thank Eglantine for that.

Mrs Procter's old English lecturer did try to identify Eglantine's story, but he couldn't find any record of its having been published before. He told Mrs Procter that it might have appeared in some magazine that doesn't happen to exist any more, but I doubt it. Personally, I think it was Eglantine's own story. I think she was an honest-to-goodness writer, who had to tell her story no matter what. It makes sense, don't you think? She wasn't murdered in our house, or buried in an unmarked grave, so what other reason would she have had for haunting us?

Oh – and there's one more thing. About three weeks after the Channel Nine program went to air, we received a call from Richard Boyer. Apparently, PRISM had been speaking to a woman who claimed that Eglantine Higgins was her great-aunt. This woman (whose name was Maureen Cameron) had seen the Channel Nine program. Although she normally lived in Queensland, she had come down south to visit a sick relative, and was keen to show PRISM some treasured family heirlooms – if anyone was interested.

Richard wanted to know if he could invite Maureen over to our house, and show her the room in which Eglantine had died.

Of course Mum said yes. She couldn't have said anything else – especially when Richard was so disappointed about the ceiling. So, one Saturday afternoon, Richard brought Maureen Cameron over to visit us, and we all sat down in the kitchen to drink tea (or cocoa) and eat chocolate cake.

Maureen was sixty-one. She told us this without hesitation when Bethan asked her how old she was. Although she had grey hair, and wrinkled eyelids, and swollen ankles, she didn't really seem *that* old – not like my grandmother. Maureen wasn't deaf or doddery. In fact she was quite sharp and quick. She had small, bright eyes that never stayed still, and she didn't miss a thing. When she was offered a piece of chocolate cake, and politely declined, she took care to add, 'Bethan can have my piece. At once.'

Clearly, she had noticed my brother mooning over the cake. She might even have sensed that sharp words had been exchanged, earlier that afternoon, over a guest's right to the first piece. The way she watched him, as he stuffed down his portion, made me think that she might have sons of her own.

'My grandmother was born in this house,'

she remarked, after we had all gathered around the kitchen table. 'But she didn't remember it very well. Her parents moved when she was quite young.'

After Eglantine died here, I thought. Mum asked if Maureen wanted to see the room in which Eglantine had very possibly breathed her last, but Maureen shook her head.

'No, thank you,' she replied. 'I didn't really come for that. I just thought that you might be interested in some of the things my grandmother saved. Some of the things she passed on to me.'

'Do you *know* much about Eglantine?' I queried. 'Do you know what she was like?'

'Not really. I know that she was bookish. Very fond of books. I suppose I take after her in that regard.' Maureen laughed a little. 'I'm a retired teacher, you see – classical languages. I'm also very stubborn, which I gather was one of Eglantine's main characteristics. Oh!' She opened the album that she was nursing on her lap, and took out a very old, very small photograph. 'I did bring you a picture of her. It's the only one I have.'

There was a general gasp. I don't know how everyone else felt, but I was awe-struck. It was like seeing a photograph of – oh, I don't know. Cleopatra, or something.

It was a brownish photograph, and it wasn't all that clear. It showed a young woman with her hair

135

piled up on top of her head, wearing a high-necked blouse and a peculiar hat. Her face was smooth and expressionless. (Mum told me later that in old photographs, the subjects had to stay still for so long that they always ended up looking like shop dummies.) I couldn't see what colour her eyes were, and her hands weren't shown, but despite this – despite her lack of expression – I got a sense of what she was like. Her face was thin, but not emaciated. Her nose was long. She had a firm chin and high cheekbones and a proud stare, and her eyebrows were very strong and dark. Only her mouth was soft.

Eglantine, I thought. Eglantine Higgins. There you are at last.

'The name Eglantine is derived from the Latin word for "prickly",' Maureen remarked, as we gazed and gazed. 'From what my grandmother told me, it suited her sister down to the ground.'

Prickly. I remembered that Michelle had described me in the same way. 'Why are you so prickly?' is what she had said. Was I really so prickly? Was I really like Eglantine?

I thought to myself, maybe I should stop criticising everything. Maybe I should stop scoffing at dumb kids and not spend so much time in the library. Maybe I should be nicer to Bethan.

After all, I don't want to end up like Eglantine.

'Do you know if she had any boyfriends?' I asked. 'I read something about how anorexia hysterica was often set off by a "romantic disappointment". Do you know if some boy dumped her, or something?'

'No,' Maureen replied. 'I'm afraid not. As I say, I don't know much about her. She did like her romantic poetry, though.'

We looked through Eglantine's album. It wasn't a photograph album, but a large book full of scraps and cuttings. She had cut poems and pictures out of newspapers and magazines. She had even pasted down a sheet of music. The song was called 'Marble Halls', and the first verse went like this:

I dreamt I dwelt in marble halls
with vassels and serfs at my side,
and of all who assembled within those walls
that I was the hope and the pride.
I had riches all too great to count
and a high ancestral name.
But I also dreamt which pleased me most
that you loved me still the same.

When I read those lyrics, I thought about Princess Emilie. And I wondered, had someone loved Eglantine? Or had she loved someone? Someone who was way beyond her reach?

It was clear that we would never know. Eglantine had managed to finish the story about Emilie, but her own story – Eglantine's story – would remain incomplete for us, because she had left no letters or diaries. We had only her album, and two stories written out in a hand that was instantly recognisable. One of these stories was completed, and it was called 'The Adamantine Tower'. The other was called 'Emilie and Osric'.

I hardly dared pick it up.

'This is the one,' I breathed. 'Look, Mum. This is it. The original.'

'Show me,' said Richard. Reverently, he turned the pages. On the last page, the writing was smeared and unsteady. It stopped in the middle of a sentence: *Beyond the* . . .

Had the pen fallen from her fingers? Had she been too weak to hold it any longer? Had she *died* shortly afterwards?

I had to blink hard, and swallow. Gently I touched the last, incomplete word.

'God,' Richard murmured. He looked up. 'You know, these documents might become quite valuable,' he said. 'There's a lot of interest in Eglantine. You might even find that someone decides to publish her stories. Some fringe publisher interested in the occult.'

'Well,' said Maureen, drily, 'Eglantine would

have been pleased about that, I daresay. Gran used to tell me that books were her passion.'

Maureen agreed that Richard could borrow Eglantine's album and stories, for a while. She also suggested that he add *Idylls of the King* to his collection. Then, at Mum's suggestion, she went outside to look at our backyard, because apparently she was something of a gardener – and when it came to gardening, Mum needed all the help she could get. They wandered out into the watery sunshine together, leaving Bethan to finish off the chocolate cake, and Ray to go back to his studio, and Richard to pore over Eglantine's documents.

I went outside too, I don't know why. I think perhaps I wanted to get away from Eglantine. Her presence seemed to hover over her album, and it was a smothering presence. In fact, it was so strong that I was half afraid she might move back into Bethan's bedroom.

She didn't, of course. She never has. Bethan pounds around there now as if she never existed; he's stuck football posters up on the walls and hung model aeroplanes from the ceiling. But we still haven't *quite* rid ourselves of Eglantine. Because as Maureen was walking around the garden, commenting on the diseased lemon tree and the unruly jasmine, and the condition of the grass, she stopped suddenly in front of a sprawling old rose bush.

120050602909　　4R7　　F/JIN

'Well, would you look at that,' she said quietly.

'What?' asked Mum.

'That rose.'

'It was here when we bought the place.'

'Oh, I can see that it must have been.' Stooping, Maureen sniffed at one of the blossoms. 'It's a sweetbriar rose,' she went on. '*Rosa rubiginosa*. The odd thing is, I've never seen one flowering at this time of year. Not ever.'

'Oh?'

'Just look how old it is. It's very, very old.' Maureen fixed Mum with her bright, penetrating gaze. 'Do you know, I wouldn't be surprised if my great-grandmother planted this?'

Mum blinked. 'You mean it's *that* old?' she exclaimed. 'How can you tell?'

'I can't. Not really. It's just something about the name.' Gently, Maureen cupped one of the fragile pink flowers in her hand, and gazed down at it. 'A lot of people don't call this sweetbriar,' she explained. 'A lot of people call this eglantine.'

Then she plucked the rose from its branch, and gave it to me.

LORETO NORMANHURST

1 2005 060290 9